FLAME

TRIALS OF BLOOD

REBECCA ROYCE

Flame

Ebook 978-1-960447-01-2

Print 978-1-960447-04-3

Hardback 978-1-960447-05-0

Copyright @ 2023 by Rebecca Royce

Cover art by Artscandre

Content Editing: Virginia Nelson

Copy Editing: Jennifer Jones at Bookends Editing

Final Proof Editing: Viv Jackson

Formatting: Ripley Proserpina

Published by Rebecca Royce

www.rebeccaroyce.com

❀ Created with Vellum

For Carol Meijers...one of the best people ever. I am privileged to know you and call you my friend.

1

Rowan's father threw me to the floor of his office. My shoulder jarred, taking the brunt of the blow as my body vibrated from the force the vampire used to shove me down. I groaned as cage doors clanged shut behind me.

Maybe cage isn't the right word? More like an enclosure. As I tried to pull myself up, my palm flattened on the floor, but heavy metal bars surrounded me, and he'd locked me inside, so it sure looked like a cage.

Shouts sounded from outside. Fredrick—who took way too much joy in shoving me around—headed to the hallway to check out the source of the noise, shutting the door behind him. They had Ace with them, and he likely wasn't coming as easily as I had. I knew better than to struggle too much against vampires, but Ace was a vampire, too. If it wasn't daytime, he might have even been able to take them on. As it was, the fact that he was awake was a minor miracle he'd rather the others not learn about. *So much for that.*

I got onto my knees and wrapped my fingers around the cool steel of the bars. For just a second, I tried to breathe.

Okay. This is happening. The elders found out about me, and it was probably somehow my fault. Maybe someone saw me at work in the store? Maybe it was the bar— *I knew I shouldn't have gone to the bar.* Was it the time I got the book for Rowan? Or when I saved Caesar? Or maybe it was when I'd been in the car with Rowan. *Hell, every time I left the house, I basically asked for this to happen.*

Letting go of the bars, I leaned my head against them instead. I never wanted to be back under the control of these people, but they addicted me to vampire venom, so what did I do instead of running as far from the blood suckers as I could? Instead of doing the smart thing, I fell in love with five of them and ended up locked in a cage.

Or an enclosure. I groaned. As usual when I'm scared, my brain focused on ridiculous little details like editing my own thoughts, but it wasn't like I knew what else to do, other than scream until my throat bled. *They'd get too much pleasure out of that. I won't scream for them. Fuck them.*

The guys could feel my pain as well as I could theirs lately. Maybe they had more opportunities to be distressed, but I knew they'd sense me as easily as I could them. They'd know I wasn't okay. Bad things might happen then. I didn't want them hurt regardless of what would happen to me. As human teenagers, I'd loved them, and they might have technically been dead for a long time, but I somehow managed to fall in love with the five people they became, too. Even though I hated vampires, I absolutely and unequivocally *didn't* hate them.

With a thunk, the door swung open, and Fredrick dragged Ace into the room, where almost all of the other elders waited. He hardly moved. By this time of day—*it has to be noon or even later now*—he wasn't even supposed to be awake.

Vampires acquired day-walking as they aged. It was unheard of for someone like Ace to even be able to do it all, but he'd risen from death with the ability. We didn't know why.

Typical. There are so many things about our situation that we still don't even understand.

As Fredrick closed the door, Ace hissed at him. It wasn't a sound I'd heard him make before. Other vampires, yes, but not Ace. My guys had been as close to human as you could be without actually being one.

Well, they'd been very human since they came back into my life, anyway.

Right then, Ace looked like a wounded monster, all traces of his humanity erased as if they were never there in the first place. His eyes gleamed red, jewel bright with blood. Even his skin was tinged rosy and his hands shook. Pain hit me fast. He needed to feed. I'd do it, if he wanted me, but it would expose what happened when we fed—and the way it turned us on—in front of their fathers.

Still, I'd do it. *Anything for Ace.*

"Explain how you're awake!" Fredrick shouted at Ace. "Explain it to me."

My guy lifted his head just a touch to regard Frederick before scooting himself as close to the edge of my enclosure as he could get. "I don't have to explain anything to you. Not ever again. You're nothing compared to me. I'm one of the reborn, remember? You worked your whole life to make sure I existed. You created us. I'd love to know how something as small as you thinks it has the right to ask a question of me."

I lifted an eyebrow. The words were downright hostile for Ace, the "good" vampire so far as I could tell. Sure, he'd been filled with rage and quasi-delusional from his inner turmoil, but he'd also been Rowan's best helper, willing to obey any command.

Frederick reared back as if he'd been struck. I tried and failed not to smirk. Okay, he also hadn't been expecting that from Ace.

All of the elders in the room had fed on me at some point or another, I realized as I scanned their faces. Well, except for Ace's father, and we still didn't know why he hadn't. It hadn't been top of my list to find out, what with everything *else* going on at the time.

In retrospect, maybe it should have been.

I reached through the bars and took Ace's hand in mine. A slight tremor shivered from his fingers, so I squeezed back. *This has to be hell for him.*

"It's going to be okay." I don't know why I would promise him that when nothing about the situation seemed anywhere near okay. Maybe it was because he would've done the same for me—once upon a time, back when he'd been human—and even though vampires didn't generally *need* reassurance, they still deserved it.

He nodded. "It is, because I'll tear them to pieces if they come anywhere near you again."

The sentiment was sweet, but I doubted he could tear anything apart in that moment. I got to my knees and dropped his hand, grabbing onto the bars so I could see the men who featured in my nightmares—back when I used to have them. My nightmares stopped one day; maybe that was when I officially gave up my hope for having a better life, since there was nothing left to frighten me.

Well, except for this very scenario. I did *not* want their mouths back on my wrist. I had to say something. Sometimes I actually could talk myself out of trouble. "So what is the problem? Is it that I'm in the state of North Carolina? I'm not bothering any of you. Why do you care that I'm here at all?"

Frederick snarled. "Rowan gave an order, and it's been broken."

I held up my hands in the universal signal for surrender. "Okay. Solid point. Let's ask Rowan how he feels about it when he wakes up, shall we?"

"I can tell you how he'll feel." Ace panted between words. "He'll want to tear you apart for touching her. Rowan changed his ruling on Maci. If he didn't tell you, that's your fucking problem, not hers. Get her out of this cage immediately."

A muscle ticked in Frederick's jaw. "If that is true, then we have a bigger problem than we realized." He looked over his shoulder. "Take your son away from here. I'll handle this as it always should have been handled. I tried it your way. Now we'll try mine."

Ace's father stared at me for a second longer. Although I only knew him as a monster who failed to protect his son from death and didn't torture me— for whatever reasons— for just a second, I could have sworn I saw pity on his face.

He nodded. "Come on, Ace."

"I'm not leaving her." Any façade of humanity vanished from Ace right then. His voice rumbled low, sounding animalistic and not at all like I was used to hearing from him.

I squeezed his fingers again. "There is nothing you can do for me right now. I know you want to, okay? I know that. I love you. I told you guys that, I think?" It was a bit of a blur. "Even if that isn't something you feel. Despite that, what you're doing right now? That feels like love to me. I need you to go with your father, and I need you to rest so you can help me tonight, okay?" I said more than I intended in front of our audience, but wanted to make sure I reached him. What he needed was to feed from me; it would make him strong. But feeding would showcase more than my words revealed, and I didn't want to go that far.

Of course, his father would make sure his needs were met by some random human. The thought burned, but I had no time for my emotional mess. Ace nodded once then rose. "Maci is Rowan's paramour. If you hurt her, there will be hell to pay."

Quite a statement, if not an outright lie. *Sort of.* I was almost all of their paramours. In fact, I was pretty sure they all would've given me that role, if I would've accepted it. But that was as close to an outright lie as I'd ever heard Ace say aloud. Technically, vampires couldn't lie—except for Ace, apparently. *Yet another way he's different.* But as far as this particular lie was concerned, if he didn't speak to Rowan before Rowan spoke to Frederick, the bad guys would know he could lie. Then he was really screwed. They'd already clued into the fact that he was still awake. If he could outright lie, it certainly wouldn't make things better for him.

He did an impressive job following his father from the room without shaking in weakness, though I knew it had to be hard for him. With a final glance back to me, he disappeared from my view. Maybe in some alternate reality he stayed and fought off every vampire in the room so we could escape together unscathed, but that wasn't my reality. In my world, Ace was a young vampire, practically unable to function past sunrise, even though he somehow could stay awake. There was nothing he could do for me right then.

Frederick's smile defined unkindness. He bent to address me. "I let you live because they backed me into a corner, but I am no longer bound by those constrictions. Now, you're mine to handle as I see fit. There is no rule protecting paramours and, besides, Rowan is too young to have a paramour. I don't know what they do with you, but it can't happen anymore. I knew who you were the second I spotted you, and I won't let you win."

He knew me? Of course he did... "You've always known me. I was just a normal teenage girl minding my business when I got sucked into your world and this nonsense. I never wanted anything to do with any of you bloodsuckers."

The click of the cage door opening was my only warning before Caesar's father hauled me out of the cell. He swung me around like a rag doll then shoved me at Frederick. "If we're doing this, let's get it done. You all might be comfortable daywalking, but I hate it, and I always have. Get rid of whatever you think she is and be done with it."

"You can't just kill me. Your son will never forgive you. None of them will. They'll destroy you for this."

Frederick shook his head and grabbed my arm. "By the time they're old enough to even attempt such a thing, they'll have long since forgotten everything about you."

Oh, I doubt that very much. It gave me little comfort, but I knew the guys were a lot more powerful than he would ever believe. *Rowan could take him down right now.*

I struggled against Fredrick's restraining grip, but it was futile. Eventually, my struggles must have annoyed him, because he whacked me right over the head. My ears rang before everything went black.

~

THEN, I died.

2

ROWAN

It was harder to wake up than it should have been. The last waking had been rough, and I'd given up the pretense of going home. Maci was in the house, awake but struggling, when I finally gave in to the dawn. I wasn't leaving the space where she resided until I put eyes on her the next waking. Hopefully asleep. Somehow, Ace could stay up. I didn't understand it. I was more powerful than him, yet he could do things I couldn't do.

Caesar moaned from his position in the bed across the room from me. We all struggled to get up. *Why?* I rubbed my arms. *What makes this night different from every other waking?*

Everything was wrong.

I threw myself out of bed and made my way to Caesar. He'd almost died in battle—*would* have died, if Maci wasn't such a fucking miracle. *Now I have to send Ace tonight to fight.* I hated it. They were my family. I didn't want to fight a meaningless war, and I didn't want them to, either.

I want this to end.

Where was Maci? Usually, I felt her the second I woke

up. Like a beacon calling me to her side, whether I needed to feed or not, she called to me. Tonight, unfortunately, I would need to feed. It would be better if Caesar could have had her alone, but we would all be hungry after what happened. Could she really handle that? She was just a human.

There was nothing "just" about Maci or our situation.

Caesar stared up at me. "Somethings wrong. I can't...feel her."

"Me neither. I'm hoping that just means she's out cold." We'd check her room. Tanner and Ace intended to stay with her. Griffin had the room to himself, and I'd bunked with Caesar in case he needed something—not that I could rouse if he did. The pretty-much-being-dead every day thing was getting old, fast.

Griffin rushed through the door as if I'd conjured him while Caesar swung his legs off the edge of the bed.

Griffin burst out, "They're not here."

"What?" His words didn't make sense. "Who's not here?"

"Ace and Maci. Tanner can't talk. I'm not sure they were here at all."

I tore into the other room, finding Tanner staring at the bed. He couldn't speak verbally, but I understood his expression completely. He was scared. *She isn't here.*

I ran a hand through my hair. "Where could Ace have taken her? The hospital? Check your phones." If she was at the hospital, I was going to freak the fuck out.

"I told her not to give me so much blood," Caesar yelled, his frantic tone matching the dull thud of my heart.

There were no messages. No way would Ace have forgotten to reach out to us. *What does it mean?* I took a deep breath. I was a vampire, a tracker. *If somehow someone came here...*

The door swung abruptly open, hitting the wall with a bang seconds before Ace's father dragged him into the room. Ace's eyes shined pure red and he raved, throwing his body onto the floor with a howl. I'd seen someone act like that once before—a vampire who needed to sleep and hadn't.

"What's going on?" I dropped to the floor to check Ace, my friend in this life and the one before. Griffin joined me soundlessly. Caesar and Tanner hadn't moved. They stared at us as if they'd been turned into statues. *What are they sensing that I'm not?*

"She's *dead*." Ace pounded on the floor, his hands fisted. Over and over again, punching as if he intended to break through the floor itself.

The sound of his thuds filled the void where my heart-beat and breath should be until I realized I wasn't breathing and gasped in enough air to speak. "What?" I rasped, still barely accomplishing sound. It couldn't be true. *No.* The only "she" he could mean would be Maci, and there was no fucking way. *No. Absolutely not.* Anger burned through me, and my vampire surged to the top of my consciousness. *Things need to break; they need to tear. We need to destroy.* To answer the impulse, I lifted the table from the floor and ripped it to pieces with my mind as if it were made of cardboard.

Everything must be destroyed. The world is demolished. It will be over today. Everything. No, Maci, no world left to give a shit about. "Let's destroy everything," I said, giving voice to the only thing my vampire would accept as suitable in the circumstances.

"On it." Griffin backed up. "Lemme grab my flame thrower. We'll start with the main house."

"Stop." Ace's father's voice rang out loud, commanding.

"It's my fault," Ace cried. "I tried, but I'm not strong enough. I tried."

Some fracture of my mind noted it was amazing he was awake at all. If there was blame to be meted out, it had little to do with Ace.

Not that it mattered. Everyone would die.

"She's coming back," his father yelled, capturing my attention. "Her father has been systematically feeding her vampire blood for years. I don't know where they dumped her, but she'll be back in a matter of months. How many? Again, I don't know, but I know she'll be back."

I tried to slow my heart rate to listen past the rushing in my ears—easier desired than done. "What?"

"You *had* to know she wasn't normal. She's like you. She was born to be reborn. It's a long story, but for now, you need to get your stuff together and run from here. Go see Warren, her father. I'll tell you how to get there, then he can explain the rest. Maci *is* coming back. She'll be different, like us, but she'll be here."

Ace hit the floor again, his rage unwavering. "He *killed* her."

Yes, he had. Our little human was fragile, and she was gone. I failed her. I tried to picture her in my mind's eye as she had been just the day before. We'd rushed her back after Caesar practically drained her dry. She'd been loopy but happy. I handed her orange juice.

"I love you." She'd smiled at the room. "Oh, I know you don't do love, but I love you. All of you."

I didn't utter a word, like my mouth was glued shut. My hands started to shake. *Vampires don't love.* But…Maci. *Oh, fuck me, I love Maci.*

And she is gone. She was coming back. That was important, and I needed to remember it so my vampire didn't slip my tethers and rain blood on the earth. But *my* Maci—the one I had known, the one I fell in love with—she was gone forever.

Regardless of whatever happened later, things would have to burn.

3

MACI

In the end, everyone dies.
Eventually.
Hopefully not too soon.
Cuz then it's tragic or something.
I have no memory of my own death.

I remember one last shot to the head by a scared man, one whose fear of losing power left him with no choice but to kill me.

So he did.

I only barely remember that happening, though. More like still frames from a movie than something that happened to me.

My guys woke up in coffins, reborn vampires with ceremony and excitement. Not that I remembered that fact particularly when I opened my eyes during my own rising. No, as I clawed through dirt and bodies, pulling my way toward the surface, I was fueled only by the aching hunger that called on me to feed. Later, I'd learn they'd thrown me in the pit where Frederick disposed of female bodies of servants he promised to change but never would. When they died, he dumped them there.

He'd thought I couldn't become a vampire, so that's where he put me, too. Just another body.

I smiled to myself. *He didn't know about the feedings.* All those years of vampire blood coursed through my veins just *waiting* to change me the moment Frederick dumped me in the fucking pit earlier than expected. But I didn't remember that then, either. I didn't know anything. Or even think that I should. All of that dulled; it fled like it didn't exist. There was nothing to think about left in my mind.

I didn't care about any of it, not really. All I wanted was blood.

So that was what I went looking for—blood.

4

The campfire crackled and spit flames. I bent over it, warming my hands while the scent of woodsmoke made me a little nostalgic. But for what? I wasn't sure.

The dead bodies were starting to cool all around me, yet I was still hungry. Then again, I was always hungry. I could put out the campfire with a bucket of water, but the fire burning a hole inside of me couldn't be quenched—not that I was sure I wanted it to ever stop. Why should I bother, when so many people just sat around the woods at night waiting to give me what I wanted?

I clenched my fists. *It isn't enough.* I frowned. But *why* was it never enough?

A noise, the cracking of a branch, caught my attention. I whirled around, ready to strike again. Were more humans just waiting to help me get through the night? I hoped so. My stomach gurgled in agreement. Hiding in their camper would be so much nicer when the sun came out if I could, for once, have a full stomach when I rested.

Five men stared at me from the other side of the fire,

appearing soundlessly from the forest near where I'd discarded two of the bodies. None of them spoke, silent in the way they regarded me and unmoving, utterly still. I wasn't fooled. They might strike at any time; they were just like me.

I bared my teeth. *This is my hunting ground*, the gesture should tell them. *I found it, and it is mine.*

The one in the center of their group nodded, as though he'd understood what I didn't say aloud. "For five nights, we've been looking for you."

Why? I didn't know them. I'd only been awake and starving for five nights. In that time, I'd done nothing to deserve their attention. They could only want the territory, and I wouldn't give it up.

"You're hungry," said the one all the way to the left. His voice resonated lower than the first one. "We're so sorry you've had to wake up alone. We had no idea where you would rise or when. We waited until we could sense you, and then we came looking. I'll *always* find you."

Nonsense. They needed to go. "Mine." It was all I could manage past the territorial spirit rising in my chest. I would make them leave if I had to, and my muscles coiled, readying for the fight.

"She has no idea who we are at all." The one all the way to the right sighed. "I hoped he would be wrong about that."

The one who they all stared at periodically—he must be their leader—appeared suddenly in my face. I reacted, shoving roughly at his meaty body. He could burn in the flames if he didn't get away from me. I'd put him in there myself, face first.

Except...he didn't budge.

"You're hungry, and we can all feel it. We can make this easier for you. Just come with us. You don't remember us now, but you're very important to us. We've waited a long time to find you. I'm Rowan—do you remember me at all?"

His words didn't make sense, especially not with the hunger making my jaw and veins practically ache with a need that the sound of his rumbly voice wasn't helping. What did he mean when he said I was important to them? *That can't be.*

I was starving. If I meant something to him, or any of them, I wouldn't ache constantly from hunger. Anyone who mattered to him shouldn't have been left in a hole to claw their way through the dirt just to feed like an animal.

The more I thought about his words, the angrier I got. The flame inside of me rose, curling white hot, far more dangerous than the nostalgic crackle of campfire. *I don't want his nonsense. Or his...untruths.* I wanted none of it. No. The hunger blinded me, leaving me panting like a dog. Finally, I found one word to speak, and I would repeat it until they understood. I pointed at the ground. *He has to understand.* "Mine."

Rowan nodded, as if I answered his question. He brushed the hair away from my forehead, and for a second, something stirred inside of me that wasn't the pangs of the need to feed that rode me constantly.

But just as quickly as it arrived, it fled, grated away by the never-ending hunger. I shoved at him once more, yet again, Rowan didn't move. "In a few weeks, when you're properly fed, you'll be stronger than me for a while, but you're not yet. Come with us, Maci. There will be plenty of blood for you where we're taking you."

No. I didn't believe them. There would be nothing there; he just wanted to take me from my place where the humans came. Besides, the sun would be out soon to burn me and force me to sleep. *Absolutely not.*

"Tanner," he said as he looked over his shoulder. "She's not coming willingly. Get her there whether she wants it or not. *Without* hurting her. The rest of us will clean up the site, like we have the others for the last five nights. Remember, we knew this would be hard."

I blinked, and the one he called Tanner appeared before me. Tanner was the only one who hadn't spoken yet. He stared at me for a long, still moment, and my monster shifted inside of me. His beast was close to the surface, like mine. I could see it there, writhing just below the edge of his steady gaze. Rowan hadn't released me, but Tanner put his hands on my arms, holding me steady for another long second before he pulled me against him. I yanked backward, trying to escape his hold, but I didn't move an inch. Through Tanner's eyes, I could see what rode me gazing back, and I stopped tugging. *He has trouble being here, too.* Like a caress, his monster touched my own. I couldn't explain the sensation if I'd been asked to, but I don't know if anyone else ever experienced such intimate knowledge.

My stomach turned, a harsh reminder of the need raking razors down my throat. I needed blood. More of it. *Now.*

Rowan dropped his hold and Tanner took over, walking as if he didn't for a moment doubt I would follow. What choice did I have? *They're taking my food away.* He was stronger than me.

Yet, as starved as I was...right in that moment, as they all stared at me quietly, I realized I'd never felt safer, not in any other moment of the five days of my memory.

Like a blip, the sensation passed. "Hungry," I repeated, trying to speak past the dryness of my aching throat.

"We know," the first one who spoke to me answered. "But not for much longer."

Pain rocketed through me, the need for more blood my only thought. Instead of giving me blood, Tanner stubbornly dragged me wherever they were taking me. I struggled, but it didn't matter.

~

AFTER THEY DRAGGED me through a house, my heels thudded on each step of the stairs to the basement where they promptly locked us inside. No buffet of humans fat as ticks with pulsing blood waited for me in the basement where they took me. The loud click of the lock moments before echoed through me like a death knell. Understanding flooded me. *They lied. There is no food here.*

"Liars," I hissed, scanning for a possible escape route.

Instead of being a proper, spooky dungeon, the vampires had brought me to what looked like a normal living room, despite it being downstairs. Couches and chairs decorated the space, as well as some clean, crisp-looking art. No people, though. No blood. No windows to escape. Way more of them and only one of me. Would they leave me here with no food? *Liars,* I thought again.

Rowan spoke past the terrified thudding of my pulse. "Never. Vampires don't do that. Well, *most* vampires don't." He shot a look toward the one who first spoke to me. "Some of us have the extraordinary ability to do so. But not me. I might deflect, but I'll never lie to you, Maci. There *is* food here." He turned and offered me his neck. "Take it."

I blinked. His words made no sense. *He isn't what I eat.* "Not right," I managed, shaking my head and trying to understand past the jarring dissonance of my thoughts.

"It is for us." His voice was low, a growling caress in my ear. "I know you think you need to feed from humans. I understand, and you're right. We do that, and you still will, I promise. But when vampires share a strong relationship—a soul- mated relationship—they can sustain one another this way. It's actually more filling and better for you. Plus, you can't kill us, not by drinking from us. Although the dead humans might not bother you now, because it never bothers any of us when we first rise, I can promise you it will eventually. Let me feed you, Maci."

He kept calling me that name. *Is it mine?*

It could be my name.

Not that I cared, I reminded myself, focusing on the neck he still offered so invitingly. I had to admit, I found his words intriguing. *Could I?* My stomach cramped. I had no choice but to try. I needed something, anything, before I died from the need.

My fangs elongated, preparing to sink into his flesh. Next to me, one of them sucked in a breath—*if they stick around, I'll eventually need names just to tell them apart.* "That is so fucking sexy," he growled.

"Ace," another one said, his tone full of censure. "We don't want to scare her."

I wasn't scared—not of them, at least. I needed to feed, but my only anxiety stemmed from the continued pain from my hunger.

Without further delay, and because I couldn't take the pain a moment longer, I closed my eyes and bit Rowan's neck. The only joy I could remember came from these moments, from feeding. I loved the way it felt to pierce the skin, the anticipation of what came next. Usually, whatever human I found screamed their head off at this point, but not Rowan. He shuddered against me, almost like...he *enjoyed* the feel of my teeth breaking his skin? His blood hit my tongue and it was my turn to gasp.

His didn't taste like a human's, that was for damn sure. This taste seemed thicker, more metallic, and it was oh-so-very warm. I sucked harder, and he shook against me. I didn't know if his knees gave out or if we both just sank to the ground.

"More," Rowan's voice rasped scratchily. "Please. Take more. All of it. I *need* you to."

I lay against him, him beneath me, and as I sucked, his body hardened. What was that? I should know. Only, I didn't, because there was just the need to feed. That was all there could be.

A hand smoothed against my back, rubbing gently. "He means it, take all of it." That was the voice of one of the guys whose name I didn't know yet. "You can't kill him. He'll pass out, wake up, feed, and then you can feed off him again. Take everything you need."

Pounding sounded in the distance, and the person talking sighed loudly. "Ace, go deal with him."

"Already on it, Griffin."

I appreciated when they used their names—helped me figure out who was who without asking. Footsteps sounded, but I decided I didn't care what was happening. Nothing mattered more in that moment than the rich pulse of blood over my tongue from this other vampire—Rowan—who I intended to feast from for as long as I could. His movements, the way he ground slightly against me, slowed, making me wonder if I truly might be about to drain him dry.

"I want to see her."

"No." I could hear the heat of Ace's anger from where I straddled Rowan on the floor. "We told you—you'll see her when we say and not before. Go away, or I'll take her so far from here that you'll never see her again. Remember, you need us more than we need you."

Idly, I wondered what was going on. Not that I particularly cared one way or the other, if I was being entirely honest. Rowan was done, not a drop left to take. I lifted my head and stared down at his calm face, his unmoving body. Would he be okay, I wondered, since I'd taken all of the blood he offered me? Would he really wake up?

Griffin touched my cheek. "He's fine."

His touch felt nice, as did the heat of the blood coursing just beneath the surface of that caress. "More."

He tilted his neck, offering me exactly what I wanted. "My turn," he said, managing somehow to sound exceptionally dominant while his pose screamed vulnerability I was only too happy to exploit.

5

I bit into Griffin's neck, eager for more. I didn't expect variation, yet I found his taste distinctly different from Rowan's. Sweeter, sort of, but darker, too. Like the bite of dark chocolate as it glides down your throat and coats your very soul in sticky goodness. *Why do I know that taste?* I wasn't sure. I couldn't have explained it; I just needed *feed*, *more*, and *now*.

One of the other ones—Ace?—still argued with a male at the top of the stairs.

"She's my daughter," the unseen voice said.

A hissing sound replied before Ace said, "You made her a pawn. You made all of us pawns, but Maci had it the worst. I don't even know where she woke up," he shouted.

I closed my eyes. *Let them argue.* The blood ran hot and wet down my throat, cool waves of peace easing the snarling pain of starvation as I swallowed more and more.

Like Rowan, this vampire also sagged, knees going soft, so I rolled Griffin beneath me, and he moaned. The low sound resonated through me, sparking nerves and swirling blissful sensations through my blood-drunk mind. As a predator, I knew information might hold later value, but I found it hard to care when I was so desperate for his blood. I sucked harder, faster than I had with Rowan, desperate to finally feel sated, full. Any insecurity about feeding from another vampire instead of a human fled. After a taste of it, I just wanted, needed, and I intended to take, greedy for more.

Another hand stroked up my back, and I writhed into the sensation—it was the one who never spoke. He rubbed steady circles against my spine, so I sucked harder from Griffin. *I need more*, my beast screamed, defying logic. Griffin's hips jerked against me as he released a final grunt, and I was sure it was over. I'd sucked him dry as well. I lifted my head—two down.

If they're lying about not dying, I hope one of them has the keys to the door in their pocket.

A pang struck me again, and it felt like concern for their well-being—*will they be okay?* I wasn't sure why I even cared. I'd never given two shits about killing humans; why should vampires be any different? Only...these vampires *were* different for some reason.

My stomach panged, pain vibrating through me as if my very veins protested. *Will I never feel full?*

I grabbed the one who had yet to speak, the one stroking my back, and pulled him down to me. His monster was close, and I wanted to rub against him. To breathe him in, to—

The feeling passed. I wanted his neck, nothing more. He tilted it toward me with a raise of his eyebrows, and my lips curled into a smile before I bit through his soft skin.

He smelled incredible, his shoulders sturdy as I gripped them to take another deep gulp. Spices flooded over my tongue, bursting like fireworks against my taste buds before sliding like silk down my throat. They all smelled so good that I inhaled just to have more of his scent inside of me.

Again, his body seemed to go boneless, allowing me to follow him to the floor.

"Maci." His voice was low, barely a whisper. Rough. His arms came around me in a hug, drawing me closer, asking me without words to take more.

Gladly, I obeyed, drawing him deep and thrilled with his willing surrender to me.

"You're right, Caesar," Ace said to the other of his group. "It worked. If she feeds from him, he can speak. It's not the blood exchange, it's Maci, just as predicted."

"She was always magic," the one he called Caesar answered, his eyes locked on me.

I couldn't remember the name of the one who didn't speak, and it bothered me even though I'd known it when he dragged me from the fire earlier. Things were clearer now, and I didn't like that error in my memory.

I pulled back. His blood dripped from my lips, and I quickly licked it up. I wouldn't waste a drop, not an ounce of it, but I needed his name. "What do I call you?"

His smile was slow. "Anything you want, but my name is Tanner. You just gave me back my voice," he added, running a fingertip across my cheek.

I didn't know what he meant about giving his voice back, and honestly, I really didn't care. I had his name. He was Tanner. I bit down again. Tanner tasted *delicious*. His loud moan vibrated through my body, so I instinctively gripped him tighter. *More*, that was all I wanted. He thrust his hips forward and a jolt of pleasure sparked up my spine. *Nice*. Some other time, I might be interested in exploring the sensation, but not when I so desperately needed to feed.

Once I finished, I gently laid the husk of Tanner onto the floor.

"Ace," Caesar spoke low. "Your turn."

He sighed. "I'm not sure I deserve it. You know what happened. This whole fucking thing is my fault."

"This whole thing is her father's fault—Frederick's fault, not yours. We've discussed this. I go last, and you agreed, let her suck you, because she's ravenous, and she will be for weeks. Hurry it up, before the sun rises. I want her as close to fully fed as possible before she goes to sleep for the night."

Did he say weeks? I got up on all fours. "This won't stop?"

Ace crossed the space between us then knelt in front of me. "Eventually it lessens, but we're always hungry. Except when...well, enough questions for now. Come on, because he's right. I don't have time to obsess, but there's always later."

I caught a movement nearby out of the corner of my eye, so I shot a look in that direction. Rowan started to roll to his side, proving they'd been right. I hadn't killed them. *That is...good.*

With a wrench of my head, I looked away. There were more pressing things than Rowan waking up. When I couldn't find the words to explain myself—my brain just didn't want to help me right then—I pounded on my chest. Finally, I managed to say, "I don't want to feel like this forever."

"I know." Ace took my hand. I was a little ashamed to see my fingers tremble in his. "But you'll get used to it. Maybe after this initial awakening, we'll be able to feed from you like you do us."

"Ace," Caesar shouted. "Too much, too soon."

Ace winced. "I'm sorry. I wasn't thinking."

"Obviously." Caesar practically groaned. He knelt to join us. "Come on, Ace is waiting. You're hungry. Deal with that, and the rest will be explained later, I promise."

I wanted answers but not more than I wanted blood. I dove at Ace, my mouth making contact with his skin as I took him down to the floor, my body on top of his. He cried out, the sound quickly changing to a sigh. He liked feeding me; they all did. The idea should be strange, but it wasn't. Mostly because I liked it, too.

His blood was warm, and it flowed easily down my throat. I almost choked on it, taking too much in a single gulp. Forcing myself to slow was hard, but I managed. His heart beat in my ears. I could hear the sound of it, so full of life and hope. Thinking back, I realized I could hear all of them, but I hadn't cared.

This was different. He was different. Awareness seemed to wash over me in a wave.

Rowan stopped to regard us as he passed us, heading for the stairs, but I didn't look up to meet his gaze. Eventually, he said something to Caesar, who only grunted in response before Rowan headed upstairs. I lifted my head. Ace was done. He had been the fastest yet. A door opened and closed. I looked in the direction of the noise to realize Rowan was gone. Where had he gone?

Caesar didn't move toward me. We weren't done. I was still hungry. I set Ace down on the ground, surprised to see a smile on his face.

The awake vampire shook his head when I glanced his way. "Not yet."

"Why?" I demanded. I couldn't take him in a fight, but they promised me I'd be fed.

"Because Rowan needs to come back before I can let you feed. I don't trust the people upstairs as far as I can throw them. I'm not sure they'll do the right thing, so one of us has to be awake at all times. Rowan can manage to stay up for ten, maybe fifteen minutes after the sun rises. So, we give him five minutes to feed and come back, then you can feed." Caesar rose and walked toward the stairs. "You can wait that long."

I thumped my hand against the floor. "It hurts."

"A temporary pain, and you should remember that. Breathe. You're strong; you always have been. You live through things that kill other people, so I know you can handle your hunger, Maci. I promise you can...and I'm sorry."

I got to my feet—they were wobbly, but I managed. "Sorry because I'm hungry but you won't feed me? Or are you sorry because of whoever it is upstairs that you don't like? My father? That's what he called the man who came down, I think. You don't like him, I can tell."

He lifted an eyebrow. "I *hate* him with a passion I rarely feel, actually. But, although I suppose I am sorry that you're hungry, that isn't why I'm apologizing."

Nothing made any sense. I had a father, and I couldn't give two shits that he existed. I only wanted what Caesar had and wasn't giving me. "Maybe he'll feed me. My father?" I paused when he frowned and shook his head in a swift, definitive movement. "Why are you sorry, then, and why not?"

"He can't feed you because only we feed you, period. End of story. And I'm sorry because I didn't find you before you rose. You awoke alone, and for that, I am sorry. I *will* always find you...only this time I was late. I felt you rise, but then it took days to pinpoint where."

He felt me rise? There was so little I understood about being a vampire. I walked toward him. "I was in a hole.

There were dead bodies everywhere. I clawed my way up, through them and through the earth." My hands were still dirty from the pulling and grabbing, actually. I stared at them as if they were foreign objects. I only needed them to grab on while I fed, so what other purpose could they serve?

I thought about the hole again. "Why *were* there so many bodies in there?"

Caesar shook his head, his lips thin before he explained. "Frederick kills women. He doesn't let them turn—major power move. He dumped you in with his victims, I guess. It makes sense, since to him, you were no different than them. I do owe your father thanks for one thing, even if it never needed to happen the way it did."

Rowan slammed the door as he entered, and I could see he stood at the top of the stairs. "Back."

Caesar needed no further invitation, and he pulled me against him. "Come on. It's almost daylight. I don't know if you know yet, but you'll be aware that it's daytime whether you're inside or out. We can feel it. You'll feed us both to sleep now. I think we have roughly ten minutes left together."

Rowan came down the stairs two at a time. "More like eight." He touched my back. "You'll get the hang of this."

I didn't want to get the hang of it. "Why?"

I hoped he knew what I meant. I didn't need an explanation of why I'd get the hang of it, not really. It was all too much.

Caesar lay down, drawing me against him, putting my mouth right where he wanted it. "Rebirth is hard. It does get easier, but no one is going to fuck with you ever again."

I bit down.

~

CONSCIOUSNESS FLOODED INTO MY MIND, the sound of low voices buzzing nearby. I wanted to bat the sound away, but the hunger forced me awake. I had to find food. *Blood. Now.*

Rowan stared down at me. "Welcome back. You're starving, I know, but you should shower first. You're covered in blood. That's normal, by the way, so not judging. We're not monsters, though, and we don't have to live like that."

Are you fucking kidding? "I need to eat first."

"It won't help. Only time will fill the ache in your stomach enough that you can otherwise function. You need the blood. We're here to give it to you as we did last night, forever. I know you, Maci. Or, at least, I did. In several manifestations of my lives, I have known you, and at no time would you be comfortable like this. You'll be glad for the shower, and then you can drain me until I'm senseless again."

I let him lead me to the bathroom, even if I was grumpy from the pain. He was right, I was a mess. A big one. And the aching inside me couldn't get worse, while I could get cleaner.

Stripping off the clothes I obviously died in felt ridiculously good. I dropped them on the floor, and only then realized I was completely naked in front of Rowan. I turned to find Rowan wasn't the only one getting a show. Ace stood next to him, and they both stared at me with obvious interest.

I turned on the water with one hand while I maintained eye contact with them. "Humans don't like to be naked."

Ace visibly swallowed then arched one brow. "Sometimes they do."

"You knew me before I was a vampire." That much had been obvious, but I found myself mildly curious. "Did I—she—like to be naked?"

Rowan's mouth twitched. "Sometimes."

I looked down at my body. I hadn't considered my appearance up until that point, not in the least. What did it matter, really? I was a vampire, and my sole purpose was to feed until I was sated. Then feed again. It seemed a wasted existence, since humans did other things.

"What is the point of any of this?"

Ace moved around me to touch the water. "Right now, the purpose is to get clean. Afterward, the only thing I'm interested in is getting you fed. Someday, not too far in the near future, you'll have other needs, other things you want to think about and do. I promise you, Maci."

Once again, I stared at my body. I had curves, breasts, hips, shapely arms and muscular legs. My stomach was flat, my abdominal muscles apparent. I was strong, and my hair was long, falling past my breasts.

"Did she look like this or has the body changed?"

They were both silent until Rowan finally answered. "In some ways, yes, in some ways, no. Mostly yes. Nothing drastic changed, but, yes, we alter physically when we are reborn."

Ace crossed his arms over his chest. "You can't remember yourself before the change?"

"Personal memories come back last for the females. It's why they're so at risk during this part. That's the excuse my father uses for what he does. Her memories will return, and she'll just know everything again suddenly. For now, get clean, Maci. You were a beautiful human and you're a stunning vampire. I could look at you naked for the rest of my life and never get bored, but we're on a deadline. Looming sun and all that, so time to get clean."

He was right, and the faster I cleaned, the faster I could eat.

"I'll stay with her," Ace said to Rowan as I stepped under the spray and pulled the curtain closed to separate myself from them. "You deal with Warren. He isn't going to stop, because he thinks he has rights. We knew he could be this kind of problem, and only you can deal with him long term."

Rowan audibly sighed. "If I let Griffin handle him, we'll have an incident. We're only here because he has the knowledge we need. I'm not convinced any of us are what they want us to be, not even Maci. In the meantime, I'm not facing Frederick blind, not while Maci is vulnerable. Until she's not, we'll stay. Afterward, as far as I'm concerned, the whole world can fuck itself and get out of our way."

Ace laughed. "Same page."

"Good. I need you, all of you. Always have. She needs blood as soon as she's out, obviously." I heard the door close, meaning he'd left, so I closed my eyes. There was so much information, and all of it confusing. *Vulnerable.*

Is that what I am? I didn't feel that vulnerable. *What a nasty word.* I was capable of doing harm to anyone and anything. I ran a hand over my body with the soap. Shampoo. I knew what that was. I used it, too. Conditioner. Dirt flowed down all around me until it stopped and finally the water ran clear. I could understand why they wanted me clean—I wouldn't have wanted to smell me either, and the thought made me smile.

I was funny. That was something I could know about myself. Maybe not much else.

I am funny.

And not *vulnerable.*

I turned off the water and flung open the shower curtain. Ace stared at me for a hot second, then dropped his gaze. He started at my feet and his gaze slowly traveled up my body, investigating every nook and cranny along the way. *Is he checking to see if I washed properly?*

As I let the water drip down me, I didn't even look for a towel. It was sort of nice to be wet. The room was warm. The yellow wallpaper might be peeling in places, but the water pressure in the shower was amazing, and the tile beneath my feet was cool, a nice contrast to the warmth of the room.

"I'm not," I finally said, since he still just looked at me.

He cleared his throat. "What?"

"I'm not vulnerable."

Ace leaned against the wall. "Would you like a towel?"

I didn't care for his non-answer. *Why does he think he can speak to me like that?* I grabbed him, ripping him off the wall, and he just smirked at me.

"Already feeling strong? I'll need to watch myself now so I don't let you take me by surprise."

He halted my pulling on him. So, he didn't want to make this easy. That was fine. I could grab him and take control, if I wanted to. It would help if he didn't expect me to do it. I kissed his neck a second before I bit it. He gasped, his arms coming around my wet body to hold on. We both slid backward with the momentum into the sink. His body hardened, particularly his cock, which pressed against me, hard. I reached out to cup it instinctively, and he groaned.

That certainly didn't happen with the humans, not in my memory anyway.

I lifted my head, licking his wound closed to save every drop of his precious blood. Ace was spicy, and I hadn't really noticed last night. I was definitely more awake at the moment.

"Normal?" I squeezed him so he'd know what I meant, and he gripped the sink on a gasp.

"With you, yes. Not with anyone else."

"Why?" I licked my lips. The answer seemed important.

He let go of the sink to cup my cheeks. "Because we belong to each other. We always have. That's why we can feed you. You'll never want anyone else now. Sure, you can still feed from humans. It's how I stayed alive the last ten months, all of us have. But we're yours and you are ours. We were always supposed to be together. And when we feed, we want more than just blood. We want sex. Because we belong to each other. When you're not so needy, you'll want it, too. Then it'll be..."

He didn't finish what he was going to say. I knew the answer anyway. "Perfect."

Ace nodded once. "Perfect. You are incredibly coherent right now. Much more than you should be."

I gripped his shirt. "I told you I'm not fucking vulnerable."

I bit down again.

When his body jerked against my own this time, I gripped him hard through his pants. If this had happened with all of them the night before, I hadn't noticed, but I was fully aware now. I stroked him. It wasn't close enough. His pants were in the way. There was only one thing to do. I tore his pants off.

Ace laughed—not the response I was going for. His blood was what I needed, but it wasn't *all* I needed in that moment. No. His underwear was in the way. It went, too. I squeezed again, this time feeling his warm skin against my fingers. He wasn't laughing anymore.

I fed, bringing his blood inside of me as I stroked him from his tip downward. One movement then another. He pulled me against him, reaching for my pussy. I stopped his hand. Another time. I didn't want it, not yet. I only wanted him to come. That was what I craved.

We stayed like that, me stroking him as I drank him down inside of myself. Minutes passed. There was just Ace and the noises he made in the bathroom. Maybe we were the only two people in existence? Right then, it seemed possible, even though I knew better.

His body jerked as he came in my hand. I smiled as I finished feeding. His body sagged against me and I held him in my arms, knowing that had been so different than it had been before.

I smiled. *Guess I actually needed that shower.*

The sound of footsteps in the hallway caught my attention. Griffin and Tanner entered the room from the bathroom, then Griffin took Ace from my arms. "I've got him."

His gaze traveled my body and shivers broke out on my skin. His neck was inviting. I almost grabbed him and bit, but I resisted...just to prove that I could.

He winked at me. "Guess we don't have to worry about your human sensibilities anymore."

I turned toward Tanner as Griffin left the room with an unconscious Ace. Tanner was once again silent. His monster was close and mine squirmed to join him. I shoved her back down. It was hard enough when she mostly left me alone. I didn't need her asserting herself more than was natural.

"Not talking again." That much was obvious.

He stared at me, so I did the same, letting myself see who he was. Danger stood in front of me, yet I wasn't afraid. I was either foolish or brave, but what did it matter when I was so fucking hungry, too?

"After I bit him—you—he could talk." I ran my hand down Tanner's neck, right over his pulse, the place I would make mine shortly. "Why?"

He wasn't going to answer me, just to let me see how far down he controlled the vampire in front of him. There was no separating them right now. I leaned over to whisper in his ear. "Is it because you know that I can protect him?"

Tanner's monster found that funny. I didn't know how I knew it exactly, but I did. A quick ripple of amusement fluttered through me. No, he didn't need me to protect him. They were perfectly strong and scary all on their own. It was something else, though. He just needed me. Tanner didn't want to be present if I wasn't. And the only way to be sure that I was there, that I was real, that I wasn't going anywhere was the feeding.

Did he want my neck? Yes, he did. For now, though, he'd wait. I blinked. We'd just had a conversation, the voiceless monster that was responsible for our rebirth and walked with us always. I smiled at him, slowly.

"Maybe someday. If I feel like it."

I grabbed his neck and bit down. *Best not to let the males think they could always have what they wanted.* It wasn't time for him to have my blood. With Tanner's pushy monster, I might have to make him earn it.

How did I know that? I wasn't sure.

He sighed when I bit. "Maci." The sound of his voice was low, like music. *He should sing sometime.* Not that very second but maybe when I wasn't so hungry. "Thank you, Maci. I need this."

I lifted my head. "You don't need it, per se. You're fine down there with him. You want it. And I want you to have it. There's a difference. Don't mistake the two."

"True." His body hardened, pressed against mine. "You should have been with us the whole time."

"I don't even know what that means." And right then, I didn't care. My moments of clarity had passed. I'd done too much thinking and not enough feeding. I was done with the bathroom.

I dragged Tanner from the room. I'd fed on the floor the whole night before and that had been great. I wasn't picky, but the beds in the other room caught my attention. I'd given no thought to my surroundings. There was a large bedroom with multiple beds. That was going to work much better than the floor.

I threw Tanner down beneath me. He wasn't fighting me at all. Would he ever? That was something we were going to have to figure out eventually if they planned to keep me here with them. Those were questions for another night. I bit down.

6

I stared down at Tanner. "Do you want me like Ace wanted me?"

"He still wants you, I can guarantee that. No past tense there. And, yes, you don't remember this, but when we were human, I took you on your first date." He took a deep breath against my neck as if he wanted to draw me inside of him. I liked that. I got wet. I loved the sensation, but I needed his blood more than sex right then. The haze of hunger threatened to overtake me again. I didn't want that. I certainly didn't know anything about when I'd been human, not even a glimmer of a memory available when I tried to find them.

I bit down on him again. His body jerked against me and, unlike the night before, I had a complete sense of what that meant. It made me smile against him. Tanner more than liked me feeding off of him. There was power to this and also a sense that I could have what I wanted when I desired it. Right then, what I wanted was his blood. It was warm, spicy, and there was an essence to it that I could now taste as Tanner. I'd never mix his blood up with Ace's; I'd always be able to tell them apart.

He dug his hands into my back, his fingers cutting me. I snarled, drinking deeper. I wasn't upset, since I liked the pain. It meant power. It was nice to have other vampires around who could dish out that kind of feeling. Allies were important and Tanner was mine. *No, that's not right, because he's more than that.* What had they said? *Soul mate.* What did it mean? I had no idea, really, but I understood blood, and I had to have that.

I sucked and sucked.

When it was over, his hands lay limp on my back. I lifted my head, licking my lips. A smile still shadowed across his face. I'd sucked him dry, and he liked it.

I wiped my mouth. Maybe it was time to find some clothes. Did I have any besides the ones I'd risen in? Someone would know. I stepped into the hallway, leaving Tanner unconscious on the bed. My stomach clenched, reminding me I wasn't done.

"Hey," Griffin said from where he leaned against the wall. "Still hungry."

He didn't ask it as a question, but he had to know I still needed to feed. Presumably, he'd been through the transition himself. I stepped toward him.

In a swift move, he touched my back, right on the cut that Tanner made. As I watched, pretty much transfixed, he brought my blood to his mouth and sucked the red drop right off his finger. I caught my breath. There was something about the intimacy of the act that I liked. I took a step closer then bit down on his neck. If he got my blood, I wanted his. His finger was still in his mouth as I got the first dose of his blood in my throat.

His body stiffened and I gasped, the world graying out for just a second.

I tensed. What was happening? Griffin was gone. In his stead, a dark landscape spread before me, the moon high in the sky, and land as far as I could see. I looked down. I wasn't naked anymore. Instead, I wore a long dress with a swooping neckline that showed off my cleavage and left my neck vulnerable. I rubbed my hand over my neck, relieved not to feel blood.

My hands...

I stared down at them. They weren't my own. They were older. Despite the darkness around me, I could see clearly that my skin was different. Usually, I was slightly olive skinned, but my hand seemed strikingly pale. Even my hair was longer, falling nearly to my waist and blonder than it should have been. I caught my breath.

I wasn't myself. Yet...I somehow was?

"Darling?"

I turned around to see Griffin, except he absolutely wasn't Griffin. He was taller, broader shouldered, and his hair fell past his shoulders. Gnawing my lip, I tried to make sense of things. Like me, he wasn't quite right, and yet, he was absolutely the vampire I knew. A sense of déjà vu overwhelmed me, almost bringing me to my knees. I'd seen this before? But when? I wasn't human, so it wasn't me remembering my human life.

I spoke, not knowing what I would say, as if the words came from my mouth because I'd already said them rather than it being a choice in the present. As though I was only along for the ride rather than steering myself, which made for a very uncomfortable sensation. "Are you okay?" I asked Not-Griffin.

"No, I'm not okay." He shook his head. "I don't know

where the others are, and we know the battle isn't going well."

It absolutely isn't. In my mind, I could picture a battle I'd never seen with my own eyes—but this version of me had. I pulled on Griffin's shirt gently, hoping to ease his worry.

"They'll be back. They're all still alive. I'd know it if they weren't." *Of course, the question was what would happen next. Warren betrayed Frederick and the others. We only knew what was going to happen because Warren had been caught. We would all have to go into hiding.*

Every vampire who wanted to continue to live in harmony with the humans, to have lives that were filled with love and not power, would have to run away. Everything inside of me abhorred the idea, but I would not lose my guys. We'd go on our next rising.

"I know." He kissed my cheek. "I wish you wouldn't step outside. It's not safe."

"Nothing is safe, but I need to be outdoors. I can't possibly be locked inside all of the time."

He sighed. "My love..."

Heat started, flames covering my body. For a second, I didn't scream. Shock flooded my system. I was on fire, and so was Griffin.

I screamed.

Rushing back into my body, I was on the floor of the house where I had been since the vampires came for me. I screamed, still feeling the bite of fire even though I absolutely wasn't on fire. Griffin did, too, apparently, writhing in agony. And just as suddenly as I ceased, so did he. He sank to the floor next to the wall, holding his head. "Damn."

Caesar picked me up off the floor and held me against him. "What the fuck happened? What's wrong?"

Rowan rushed over, squatting between Griffin and me. "Explain."

I didn't have the slightest idea what happened, so I couldn't answer him. Instead, I just trembled in Caesar's arms. I'd been on fire, my skin burned from my body. I shuddered remembering it, and how it felt.

"It happened." Griffin still hadn't moved from where he was on the—floor, and his voice sounded rough, as if someone put his voice through a cheese grater. He probably felt the skin flay from his body as well. We shared that, assuming he had been there too. I didn't really know for sure how any of it worked.

"I need blood." I managed to crack out my request before I started to shake violently. My head clouded over. There was only the need to feed. Everything else had been too much.

"Here." Caesar gave me his neck. "Take it. Whatever you need, Maci." He petted my hair as he extended his neck lower. "Take it. Always."

I bit down. Their voices drifted over me while I closed my eyes. I'd done too much. I just needed to feed, nothing else.

"I took her blood," Griffin explained to Rowan. "And then she drank from me. Suddenly, I was in his body—you know, the one I'm supposed to be reincarnated from or whatever. The guy they kept expecting me to be, but I wasn't when I rose—like all of us, but I *was* him. And she was there, too. She was that woman, the one her father wants back. It worked. We really are who they think we are. *Fuck*."

I closed my eyes, still feeling the bite of flame. I didn't want to be her. It hurt too much.

"Maci," Griffin's voice called, and I lifted my head. Truthfully, I had no idea how long Caesar had been unconscious beneath me, but he was. I drained him a while ago.

Only Griffin might understand me. "It hurt."

"I know it did. It mostly hurt to watch that version of me burn." He pulled me off Caesar. Ace came up the stairs, his pallor grayer than usual, and he shot us a look I couldn't understand. "Come on. Let's get you in some clothes, then you can feed from me. You must still be hungry, and Rowan wants to go last before bed."

Griffin didn't strike me as cuddly, but he held me in his arms like I was important to him. "You felt it, too? The burning."

He nodded once. "I did, but the rest of it was great. It really was. I'm not him, but I feel better for knowing him."

I lifted my head. "The rest of it? The two-minute conversation we shared? That wasn't so fantastic. It was mostly stressful."

Griffin's mouth fell open like a landed fish. "That's all you saw? At the very end, I saw their whole relationship."

"Why would you see more than I did?"

"I don't know." Rowan paced the room. "But we didn't know that you two sharing blood at the same time would trigger anything either, so obviously we're all in the dark, and no one knows jack shit."

Dark amusement had me smiling. "Does he curse a lot?"

"No," Griffin replied with a laugh. "I'd say the circumstances we're all in warrant the words though. Like I said, I saw the whole relationship, and the burning still sucked. Must be awful for you."

I shuddered at the memory. "Not doing it again."

"Only he was with you when you burned. You won't see that again, I don't think. Come on, Maci, feed. You need it."

Griffin didn't understand, so I tried to explain. "If that's how we die, if that's what happens to us, then why are we doing this at all? Why even be vampires? Why do we bother with any of it, if it all just ends up like that? We'll end up screaming as we die no matter what."

Griffin shrugged. "That's the nature of life for all beings, I think. I don't believe most living creatures enjoy their eventual end. We all had a terrible first death. Maybe you don't remember yours, but I remember mine. It sucked. The good news is we all got a second chance—maybe a better chance. I wouldn't be human again. I prefer being a vampire."

Rowan stopped pacing to point out, "It's not just flames. We could be beheaded. We could be staked. There's lots of ways to die."

Griffin groaned. "I don't think you're helping."

"I'm not trying to help, I'm trying to explain. She doesn't know everything about our lives yet. I want to make sure she's fully informed. We all need to see like you did, Griffin. We have to. Otherwise, Warren will use us the way that Frederick used them."

That name rang a bell for me. "I heard that name in the vision. Warren betrayed them or something."

"Yes, he did." Rowan approached me slowly, squatting down. "And Warren is upstairs right now. He's not supposed to be. He's supposed to be in his own house, but he refuses to leave. He's your father, Maci."

That makes no sense. "He was absolutely not my father in that...memory or whatever it was."

"No, he wasn't." Griffin sighed. "It's complicated. How about we agree to talk about it tomorrow? Answers tomorrow, and tonight, you need to feed."

He was right, and truthfully, right then, I really didn't care that much. I didn't give two shits about the person whose memories I had. What happened to her? Not my problem. I knew just how to solve my problems…

I bit down on Griffin's neck. He sighed and leaned back as if he'd been waiting for my bite.

This is all that matters. Only blood counted for anything.

Sometime later, Rowan lifted me from Griffin. "Come on. Feed us both to sleep. Tomorrow is soon enough to figure things out."

"I don't want to do that. I don't care. I'm not sharing blood if I have to go through that again."

He sighed. "You don't have a choice, Maci. We were born without a lot of choices and reborn that way, too. But we also have certain things, certain people, that others don't have. For that, I am actually enormously grateful. You're not supposed to be cognizant enough to even discuss any of this right now, but you always defied expectations. Some of it, I understand. Some of it, I don't, but I'm glad to be here with you while we figure it all out. If I could go back and answer something your human-self said to me, I would, if I could."

I swallowed and blinked fast, not sure why tears threatened to fall. Why was I upset? I hardly understood a word he said to me. Still, I pressed on the thread I could follow. "What did she say to you?"

"That she loved me. All of us. She said it."

I dwelled on that for a second as I turned over to reach Rowan's neck. "How lovely for her to have loved."

"I suppose that's one way to look at it." He tilted his neck to give me better access. "Bite me. Put us both to sleep. Can you feel the sun coming?"

Maybe. His pulse called to me, so I bit down instead of answering him.

I WAS ONCE AGAIN the last to wake. *How do they all get up so much earlier?* I had no idea the world existed until my eyes flew open every rising. What got them up so much faster?

Ace sat on the floor next to me and explained. "It comes with age. I can stay up past sunrise when I'm not drained of blood." He winked at me. "Your question was written all over your face. Come on. Go take a shower, put on some clothes. I left some for you in the bathroom. If you're up for it, we'll try to talk about things with you that aren't about blood. We haven't gotten to do that with all five of us awake at the same time as you."

It was an interesting thought. My monster paced impatiently inside of me—she didn't want to talk about anything. She just wanted to feed. Tanner stepped forward, taking my hand. He wasn't talking again, but I could understand him just fine. His monster was present, too, and if I wanted, we could be purely animalistic together. The thought was appealing.

Still, I walked to the bathroom, letting my hatred of existence show all over my face. What was the point, if I had to feel like this every time I woke up? I washed quickly. The shower was less exhilarating, but maybe simply because I didn't have to wash off death, dirt and blood. Instead, my muscles ached. I felt stronger killing the humans than I did feeding from other vampires—although that hadn't been the case before I'd been thrust into those memories, so maybe that was the problem, since the guys tasted so much better than the humans. My mouth watered at the memory.

Turning off the shower, I dried off and got dressed. Ace left me some soft black pants and a black t-shirt that didn't quite cover my belly button, so part of my stomach showed. They didn't leave me socks or shoes, but I was mostly dressed.

The heat from the steam of the shower followed me when I walked back into the main part of the basement.

They all waited and turned to regard me when I entered, but not one of them spoke. They were worried about whatever it was that they had to say, I realized. How did I know that? Had my human-self known them so well that part of what she knew passed onto me? *Maybe.*

"Say it." I didn't pretend I couldn't read them, calling them out on their silence.

Rowan rocked back on his feet. "I promised you answers, and you're going to get them. The vampires alive today are warring. Warren, your father, and his friends—which also includes Ace's father—are against my father and some of the others. A prophecy was discovered some time ago, back when some part of you was alive in another vampire. It said that those particular vampires—the one you saw, Griffin's, the rest are ours, I presume—would reincarnate, and that we would help win a war for whichever side controlled us."

My head pounded. They hadn't fed me yet, so it was a lot to digest on an empty stomach. I tried to concentrate despite that, but it was a struggle to remain focused.

Rowan kept talking, seemingly unaware of my struggle. "My father was convinced that leaving you out of it was the way to go. He didn't like you when they were all alive at the same time, so he mastered things—and he killed any woman who was pregnant with a girl. Your father took advantage of his surety that a girl child would be his undoing. On his end, he made sure his human got pregnant with a girl—you. But we weren't raised together, and you didn't know anything about vampires or any of it. He didn't raise you himself, and instead he sent you away so you'd eventually find us. And you did."

Ace finally interrupted. "But your asshole father didn't

leave things alone even at that point. He kept feeding you vampire blood, so if you died, you would change. He kept us all in the dark in regard to his plan, of course. He had his reasons, and he doesn't elaborate on that part. So now you're here with us as a vampire, and none of us had our extra memories until yesterday."

The fire. I shuddered. "I don't want to burn again."

"I don't think you will, because only Griffin saw you burn. Any blood you exchange with me can't show you something I wasn't there to witness," Ace supplied, rocking back on his feet. "It's too much to ask you. You don't even have your human memories yet. We aren't going to be used by either side. Right now, we're here with your father because he has what we need—information. It doesn't have to be that way, but for now, we have to know what he knows."

"To keep you safe," Caesar explained in a low voice. "I'm not running anyone else's war, but we have to know how we can best control our own lives. Fuck all of the rest of them."

I understood finally what they were saying. "You need me to share blood and to go through all of that again. Maybe not burning, but who knows what I'll remember, so I have to go through that again whether or not I want to. I have to do it so that you can all have the information you need to keep going."

Silence hung heavy in the room for long moments, no one answering me, until finally Griffin did. "You need the information, too. Frederick killed you, by the way. With no intention of you being reborn, he just killed the human who bothered him because he hated that woman. Why? We don't know. I'm not even sure that I know, and I have all of that guy's memories. I only have the sense that he absolutely hated her. What did she do to him? We need to know that."

I lifted my chin. I wouldn't be threatened. "You'll deny me blood if I say no?"

Tanner jolted. He couldn't speak, but he grabbed my hand and put it over his heart. His monster met my gaze. No, he wouldn't deny me blood. He'd *never* do that.

Why? It would be the logical way to make me comply.

Caesar strode over and placed his hand on my cheek, cupping my face gently. "It needs to be your choice. We can't make you do anything, and we won't starve you. We'll feed you forever. You're ours. I'm hoping when you gain clarity, you'll remember that. You can think about it in the meantime. Nothing has to be done today, or at least not all of it. Whatever way you want to do it, we'll do it. I can't pretend to understand what you went through in that memory. I do know my own death, and I know I wouldn't relive that on purpose. We'll take our cues from you, but we're all in agreement, it would be best for this to happen."

"Well then, let's not put it off." I didn't need it hanging over my head. "Let's get the pain over with, since that's all my life is anyway."

Rowan held up his hand. "Hold on. That isn't all your life is, and if you feel that way, then that's the first thing we can fix. Come on, enough of this basement." He took my hand in his. "We're going upstairs."

"Is that safe for her?" Ace was quick to follow when Rowan pulled me up the stairs. "We've locked the world out for a reason."

"She's a vampire. Maci can defend herself pretty well, I would imagine. Besides, I don't think Warren wants to hurt her. He wants to *use* her. Griffin, I charge you with doing something about that tonight."

He laughed. "I love fucking with Warren."

"I know you do." Rowan's grip was strong in mine while

he keyed in a code to open the door at the top of the stairs. I pulled my hand free, stopping him from moving onward. "What's wrong?"

I pointed at my feet. "I don't have shoes."

"That's okay. We're only going to step outside for a second. You have strong, vampire feet. They won't get hurt from a moment shoeless." He kicked off his own shoes. "There, we'll do it together."

The sound of the others kicking off their shoes made me smile. They were sort of...cute. "I need to feed," I reminded him.

"I know." Rowan squeezed my hand and pulled me into the hallway. I hadn't really made note of the house when we arrived, so I scanned the building. The doorway opened onto a huge front hall, with massively tall and oppressive ceilings. To the left, the hallway opened into a living room that looked comfortably situated. The right opened into a large, industrial sized kitchen—which was funny in a vampire household. It wasn't like they ate.

That was when I smelled them...*humans.* I caught my breath. I preferred feeding off the guys, but there were humans nearby, and they smelled so edible. My stomach clenched, a painful cramp grumbling through me in a wave.

Ace put his arm around my shoulders. "Ignore them. You don't need them."

"Why are there humans here, and why couldn't I smell them from downstairs?"

He shrugged, the movement jostling both of us. "Maybe you can only smell us, babe."

Griffin groaned. "And Ace dives into the cheese this early into the reintroduction."

Rowan opened a porch door and gestured for me to follow him through it. The wind blew through the opening, cooling off the room significantly. Rowan held my hand as we stepped into the night, and the breeze pushed away the scent of the humans. Instead, all I could smell was the wild and trees. I closed my eyes. I hadn't loved the smell of the earth when I'd been running around trying to survive, but tonight, it was breathtaking.

And alive.

The world was filled with sounds. Crickets. Birds. A car horn in the distance. The wind looped around my head—a gentle breeze, but it felt like so much more. And the colors everywhere. Everything seemed more vibrant and detailed than I remembered.

I lifted my head. "This is...so much better."

"We're not meant to be locked inside." Rowan's voice was low. "It's necessary right now, but that isn't how we live. This is how we exist. Our lives aren't pain; they're filled with purpose. I didn't understand that myself, not until there was you. Caesar knew. He woke up knowing that you were our reason. It took so much longer for us. I'm grateful to him for finding you. I'm elated that you're here with us, even if how it happened was hell for you. I just need your buy in, Maci. Can you trust us to get through this with you?"

My skin tingled. There was life out there, and my heart clenched at the thought of leaving the five of them. He didn't need my buy in. He'd had it from moment one, even if I hadn't understood why and still didn't, really. "You need to feed from me. If we're going to do this, let's not keep hiding."

7

"Come on." Rowan gestured with his hand. "You need to feed, and there's absolutely no reason you can't do it out here in the night, with only the moon watching."

I lifted my gaze to stare at the celestial body he mentioned—partially hidden by clouds and not full, but still lovely. I smiled at it. "Well..."

I never got to finish whatever I was going to say. Tanner rushed to me, stopping in front of me. We stared at each other for a moment, our monsters greeting the night. We weren't just humans in another form; we were predators. I could see it right there in Tanner's gaze, the needs that would always be there. I didn't have to hunt humans—but that didn't mean I didn't want to. Perhaps not craving humans was another skill I'd slowly get a handle on, but I didn't have it yet.

Tanner grabbed my arm. What did he want from me? But then it dawned on me. He wanted me to catch him, to find him. I yanked out of his grip on my arm and nodded. We could do that. He rounded on Rowan—Tanner couldn't talk, but Rowan must have understood him. Their leader—and that was clearly what Rowan was—stepped back, putting his hands in front of him. "I won't interfere."

With that, Tanner ran past me faster than I could believe was possible. *Oh wow.* My body tingled with anticipation. My bare feet forgotten, I took off running. I'd never been to this place before, but I felt like I knew it because I tracked Tanner. It wasn't about where we were going anyway, just about what I chased. My mouth watered, and my head buzzed.

Yes, I'd been made to do this. I needed it.

Tanner was fast. I'd catch a glimpse of his dark shirt, and then it would be gone. I couldn't go by sight, not with prey so much better at running than me. He'd been living with his monster a lot longer than me, so they were more in sync.

That was the answer. I had to stop thinking like a human and just, for a few minutes, trust my vampire self. It was the only way I could use my beautiful monstrous strength to catch Tanner and give us both what we needed. My thoughts fled, my mind only interested in the smells, the noises, and the ease with which my body moved when I wasn't fucking thinking about it. I ran, not sure if I was doing the right thing or not. It didn't matter. I knew I could catch him. I was just that good.

Time had ceased to matter when I finally spotted him. He made the wrong turn and, for just a second, was clearly in view. I rushed forward and took him straight to the ground. He went down with a thud, my mouth on his neck before I let my brain turn back on. I wasn't gentle, but he didn't seem to mind. The sound of his sigh, filled with pleasure, made me smile as I sucked down his blood. I needed it and what was clear was that he wanted it.

"Maci. " He sounded like he was smiling . "Thank you.

For catching me. For this. For all of it. We're vampires. We live at night, but our lives are not dark. Now that you're here, there isn't any more bleak. Feel that, too."

I did right then.

I took what I needed.

CAESAR RUBBED blood off my chin. We both sat with Tanner while he slept off what I'd done to him. We weren't in the basement, and he couldn't just be left outside, where anything could happen to him. Particularly not since I was fully aware of the fire issue—one match and he was gone.

I wouldn't lose him. Not any of them. Whatever else I didn't know, I understood that fact perfectly. They were mine, and a surge of protectiveness rippled through me. I couldn't lose them, not again.

"You're all torn up," Caesar said as he picked up my foot. "I'll get you some shoes."

I shrugged. "It didn't hurt."

"Honestly, it looked exhilarating. I'd ask you to chase me, but I can't have you out of my sight long enough to disappear from my view."

He swept his finger over my bleeding foot. "May I?"

I tilted my head. "Are you actually asking?"

"If I take your blood and then you feed from me later, you'll get zapped back into that other person's memories so, yes, I'm asking. Griffin fell into it by mistake, but now that we know it can happen, you'll get a say before you are forced into experiencing that again."

Caesar seemed very focused on keeping me safe, so I figured it might be left over from his feelings for my human-

self. I couldn't think of any other reason he'd want that jour-
ney, not unless he really thought it was the best way to
prevent something from going wrong.

"Go ahead. As soon as Tanner's up, we'll jump in, so to
speak."

"Tanner's up," the vampire himself said, and I noticed he
leaned on his elbows. "I'm good. I'm going to go find a
human to take care of my hunger, then we'll move forward.
Caesar doesn't have to babysit me another minute."

I laughed. "It was actually my idea."

"Nonsense. He might have let you think that, but Caesar
is our watcher. He's good at it, takes care of everyone. He
went along with it being your idea, but I promise, if you
didn't think of it, he would've."

He stood, brushing off his jeans. "That was fun. You
caught me fair and square. I didn't let you do it."

What a ridiculous notion. "Of course I did."

"Is that my daughter?" I didn't recognize the voice, so I
turned in time to see Griffin blocking another man's
entrance. *Warren*...that had to be him. I stood, brushing off
debris from my own legs. If I was meeting this person, I
wasn't doing so from a position of submission. Caesar stuck
his finger, the one dotted with my blood, in his mouth. For a
second, he closed his eyes. I guessed he liked the taste.

Griffin shook his head. "Not until we say yes. In fact,
pack your stuff and get out of our house. Go home. When
we're ready for you to see her, you can see her, but not a
moment before."

Warren pointed at me. "She's right there! At least let her
see her mother. The woman has waited almost two decades
to see her."

They hadn't said anything about a mother. I never

thought about having one of those, although I suppose everyone did. I didn't just pop out of nowhere into existence with only a father. At some point, I'd been human, which required a father *and* a mother.

"She's not her mother. None of you behaved as actual parents and, you know what? That's fine. Vampires make terrible parents. We all had the worst of parents as humans, but what you two did to that human girl was deplorable. Even if she's fine now—strong and beautiful—what you did to her when she was a baby is irredeemable." Griffin practically snarled, "*You* wanted this. *You* wanted us to be here. *You* betrayed and hurt people to ensure we showed up. Well, here I am. Think you can take me? Want to try?"

I could actually smell his anger in the air. It tasted bitter, acidic on my tongue. Strong emotions had different scents, some of which smelled or tasted different, even though it was the first time I encountered it.

Caesar smiled, but no mirth glinted behind his eyes. "When Griffin gets like this, it's incredible. He doesn't usually fight, because he's more of a thinker than a brawler. But when it comes to you? All bets are off. Rowan was smart to sic him on Warren. When you're only willing to kill for one person, you're willing to go to extremes. We're the same that way, and we're all devoted to you. Know that."

Warren met my gaze, despite the distance separating us. "I'm your father, Maci."

I turned my back on him. I didn't have all the information I needed to deal with him just yet. I wasn't ready. If Griffin and the others didn't want me talking to him right then, I'd trust them, so I wasn't going to do it. Why fight for the purpose of fighting when I was sure there were more meaningful battles to come?

"Remind me not to piss you off," Tanner said as he

walked away, presumably to go feed. My stomach panged. I really didn't want him feeding from someone else, but what was I supposed to do about that? I needed to spend some time actually focused on the problem—they couldn't keep feeding from humans. They were mine, but we'd be in a constant circle of feeding, with one of us always draining the others, wouldn't we?

Warren left as well. The air moved better without Warren there, but without Tanner, it felt emptier. Caesar pulled me to him. "Would you be okay if we went inside to feed? I don't like how exposed we are out here."

Griffin laughed. "I wouldn't let anyone get to you, Caesar, but that's fine by me. Go inside. Have some private time with our girl. We need to move upstairs and figure out what to do about the humans in the house. We need them to feed but...yeah, I don't want to keep her in the basement forever."

Regardless of who I might have been before I awoke as a vampire, I awoke as someone who didn't give a shit about planning or logistics. They could work the details out any way they wanted, since I didn't care where I passed out for the night.

I threw a final glance over my shoulder. It was probably best if I couldn't see Tanner feeding off a human. I might snap the person's neck, unable to resist the urge.

Caesar led us into the quiet house. The smell of the humans had dissipated, which meant someone moved them outside. Obviously, the guys needed food nearby to keep up with my waking hunger, but I hadn't considered the logistics at all. Not that I had answers as to what to do about it.

"What's the matter?" Caesar led me to a bedroom on the second floor. Fortunately, it didn't have the scent of having been recently occupied, which I found I desired. I lived basically in the dirt surrounded by dead bodies just days ago, so why did it bother me? Had I been suddenly domesticated?

I tried to find the words to explain something I didn't fully understand myself yet. "I don't like you guys feeding from humans. I understand the need, I'm just explaining what's bothering me."

He brushed my hair away from my face. "You are days from changing. At this point, I was raving, either trying to eat all the time or thinking about you. I was incoherent, a lunatic, starved. You're having *conversations*. It won't be forever that you can't feed us. We'll actually be constantly feeding each other, because we don't need as much when we're with you. Just a bit, then you'll feed off someone different. None of us will be starved. You'll be full all the time, that's how we'll work this. For now, yes, we have these humans. They want to be here, because they want to be vampires. Unlike Frederick, Warren'll actually make them vampires afterward."

Very interesting, but his explanation did nothing to soothe my jealousy nor my desire to destroy whoever Tanner touched. I smiled at Caesar, but I imagine the expression held about as much happiness as his earlier baring of teeth. "If you're expecting reason from me, you're going to be immensely disappointed," I finally replied.

"I'm not expecting anything from you except for you to be yourself."

They acted like they all cared for me, but none of them knew me, not really. I didn't even know myself yet. "Who was she? The human that wore my body that you all liked so much."

He sat down on the bed, kicked off his shoes, then leaned against the headboard. "I didn't just *like* her. I was obsessed with her. I needed her more than anything in the universe. Although I made the error of my vampire life by not telling her, I loved her very much."

His words made me catch my breath. I wasn't sure why, but my face felt hot, and my heart beat a little harder. "What was your reasoning for not telling her, if she mattered that much to you?"

He offered his hand, and I easily linked my fingers in his, allowing him to draw me closer. "Because I thought vampires didn't love, so I didn't believe what I felt for her could possibly be love."

I snorted. "Yet somehow you've learned differently in the time since she died?"

We were so close, practically mouth-to-mouth, so I took the initiative and kissed him. I needed to feed, but I wanted to know what his lips felt like touching mine. He closed his eyes and didn't press for more when I moved away, missing the warm embrace of our linked lips the second it passed.

"I did." He answered my previous question. "First of all, I didn't know vampires had soul mates until her. Once I understood why I couldn't do without her, why I needed her to feed from, that I loved her? And then to experience the nine, almost ten, long months she was dead, and you weren't here yet? It was hell. So, yes, I learned a lot about my feelings since she died. They're lessons I won't readily forget." He lifted his lids. "You need to feed. I can feel your hunger. Feed, Maci. I know you, even though you're about to tell me I don't. I do, so feed and don't argue for now."

I couldn't help but smirk. "Don't you want to have sex with me, Caesar?"

"So much, Maci." He bit my lower lip. "After you feed."

I rubbed against him, but I said, "You're going to travel if I feed. We both will."

Caesar leaned over to kiss my cheek, lingering there.

"Then we'll have sex afterward. You'll bite me, feed a bit. You'll travel, come back, feed until you're almost full...but stop before I'm knocked out. We'll have sex, then you'll finish feeding."

My smile was slow this time. "You like to be in charge."

"Only when it comes to you and how I want things to be. I don't give a shit what happens otherwise."

I had similar thoughts myself earlier. "Okay."

"Thank you."

I bit his neck, and not gently. He groaned, which turned out to be the last noise I heard before I was thrown backward into the memories of the other person who apparently lived in my head. I hadn't asked for any of it, I didn't want it, and there wasn't a thing I could do to stop any of the things happening to me.

If there was someone to complain to, I would complain about the absolute lack of control life gave me, but sadly, even vampire life apparently came without anyone who gave a shit.

"What are you doing?" the man who was Caesar but wasn't asked.

I extended my arms toward him, and he crawled into them, nuzzling against my neck. He was the most affectionate out of all my guys and would like what I had to say the least. "I think this is the end."

"Why? Why now?" He lifted his head. "Frederick isn't garnering *that* much support."

He hadn't seen what I had the day before. He didn't know. "He is. They like the idea of power, of living on their own terms, of owning humans. They don't want to search for soul mates, and they don't want to follow the rules. I heard people chanting their support of him. And then he said anyone who disagreed needed to be killed." I sighed.

"He looked directly at me. I thought about killing him right there."

"I would have, and I wish you had." He closed his eyes. "I won't let them hurt you."

I shook my head. "We have to talk. Seriously, sit up."

With a grumble, he lifted his head and raised an eyebrow. "What?"

"I think this is ending. I also think the prophecy is very concerning. They say those people will die, but then they'll be somehow reborn at the same time? Do you think it could be us?"

He took my cheeks in his hands and smoothed his thumbs under my eyes. "You need to feed. You'll feel less filled with doom if you do."

He might be right, but I growled at how easily he dismissed my words as a need to feed. I shoved at him. "You're not listening to me, and I'm not to be dismissed. Out of everyone here, I'm the most intuitive. I might not see prophecies, but I'm strong in our powers. Due to that, you should listen when I tell you we're in big trouble."

They liked to baby me, to make sure that I was happy, that I had everything I wanted. Most of the time, I even felt like they listened to me and valued me. On this subject, though, they couldn't seem to see the threat Frederick posed.

"If we don't take this seriously, we'll all regret it."

I jerked back into my body at the same time as Caesar, because he grabbed his head the same way Griffin did after he saw those other vampires. My head didn't hurt, thankfully, but both of my men showed signs of pain after the vision.

He pulled me against him roughly until we panted

together, not once allowing me to look away from him. "I saw his entire life. How much did you get?"

"Just a long moment." I swallowed, my mouth going dry when I smelled a familiar scent. Blood leaked slowly from the wound on his neck. We hadn't been under for very long.

He rubbed my hair from my forehead. "Which moment? They shared so many."

"The one where she begged him to listen to her and he didn't."

Caesar frowned. "Not his finest moment, that's for sure. Trust me, she was right, and he regretted it. They arrived home just in time to see you and the one I think was Griffin burn. It was absolute hell, but none of that matters right now. Let's assume you're seeing the things that you need to see in this whole fucked up situation. If that's true, you saw how we didn't listen to her. Because of it, she burned to death with the one who wasn't Griffin. The rest of us saw them die, and then we died terribly afterward. I'll admit, you seeing that moment feels like a big warning sign, and I'm not an idiot."

I hoped that was true. If not, and if our history was just bound to repeat, then what was the point?

"Look, I'm not dismissing the topic or the conversation, but you must be fucking starving."

He wasn't wrong, but it wasn't what I wanted just then. I licked the blood off his neck, reveling when Caesar shuddered beneath me. I kissed his chin and then his mouth. "I'm going out of order, but I want to fuck you now, Caesar. I want to feel alive in this body, like it's not just hers. And I don't like being chained to my stomach. I'll feed when I want and not otherwise. That's what I got from that experience—I'm not going to waste time feeding when I should be doing other things."

Beneath me, he caught his breath. "Whatever you want, Maci. Feel alive in your beautiful vampire body."

I tugged off his shirt, revealing his muscled skin beneath. I had questions for them later. There were so many things about being a vampire I didn't understand. Were we this strong when we were humans? Did it matter? Caesar's body attracted me, but not as much as his self-confidence and the way that he looked at me—as though the world moved because I was in it. Those things were the real turn on.

Or as much of one as I apparently needed. I wasn't particularly concerned with physical beauty—I preferred strength—but Caesar was a gorgeous man. I traced along the smooth skin over the bumps of his abdominal muscles with a fingertip. I wanted to bite him there... *Maybe another time.*

He tugged at my shirt, pulling it over my head. "I liked it when you were walking around naked. That was the best, but we wouldn't want other people to see you that way. Your nakedness belongs to us."

I grinned at him. "That seems very human of you, Caesar."

"Well, we can blame you for that."

He flipped me over. I caught my breath. I guessed I wasn't going to be in charge all the time, which was more than fine by me. Caesar—*hell, all of them*—were strong males. I could tell by watching them, taste it on my tongue in their presence, it practically took up its own separate sense. They let me be in charge, but that's all it was—them letting me.

I need to remember that.

Maybe I shouldn't have found their superior strength so sexy?

"Fast." I didn't want to wait. I was wet and achy. I needed

to be fed, but another part of my body felt neglected since my rebirth and proved just as anxious to find completion.

"Tsk tsk." His smile was slow and all-consuming. "This is my show. You don't tell me how it will go."

I bit down on my lip, thinking about making him bleed, and not because I wanted to feed. There was power in blood. I could take it back. Maybe.

"But it is my pleasure to give you what you want." Caesar grinned, and his toothy smile spoke of ownership. That was okay. I already knew, in the brief time we'd been together, that the opposite was also true. I owned him as much as he did me.

And he was more than fine with that.

He tore my clothes from my body. I wanted him as naked as me, so if he could tear, so could I. With a yank, I removed his clothing with a satisfying ripping noise.

I might not remember being human, but I must have been weak, because I reveled in my strength. He flipped me over easily, so I grabbed onto the headboard. I wanted the moment, and I wanted to share it with him.

He rose up behind me, the sheets pulling up against my skin with his movement. Caesar palmed my breasts in his big hands, and I gasped. My nerve endings sparked to brilliant life, leaving me wanting more touch, as much as I could possibly get.

"More," I demanded as the thoughts slammed around in my head.

"Plenty more to come," he whispered in my ear. One of his palms streaked down my body while the other one squeezed, applying slow even pressure to my breast in his hand. I sighed. Yes, gentle slow movement, the best sensation in the world.

Caesar pressed a finger inside of me. I clenched my

muscles around him writhing, into his touch. "More," I whispered again, my voice practically wobbling in my need.

He leaned over and pressed his nose against my neck. "I know what you need, Maci," he promised as he pushed his cock inside of me.

8

I gasped. Yes, I wanted more. As much as I could have. Needy heat rippled down my body, an ache between my legs building with each slide of his skin against mine. Caesar couldn't hurt me. There was just so much pleasure in the bites of pain where his fingertips pulled me closer. I closed my eyes and rode the waves as they hit me. I moaned and yelled, I even screamed, begging him for more. Nonsense words, but I had to give sound to the sensations flooding my body. His grunt in my ear, as he thrust balls deep inside of me, was the best sound I'd ever heard.

I came around him, all the tension of the day releasing in one instant of pleasure I knew I'd never forget. He came with me—with a hard jerk, Caesar was, in that second, entirely mine. After a moment, he pulled out of my body and flipped me over.

I groaned. I liked how full I felt with him inside of me. My body still throbbed where he'd been only moments ago.

He kissed my mouth, grinning against me. "That was insane."

"Not the word I would've used, but I suppose it'll do." I

wrapped my arms around his neck, surprised by how much I wanted to just snuggle against him. I didn't think I was a clingy person, but it seemed right then, I absolutely was.

"What word would you have used?" He kissed my cheek. "Amazing?"

I smiled, slowly. "I guess I can't use one word. I'd say it was just what I needed."

He nodded. "Absolutely." He fell quiet for a moment and then stroked a hand over my hair. "What was it like? I want to know what waking up was like for you."

He wants to discuss that now? "Why?"

"I searched. For the ten months you were gone, I never stopped looking for you. I'd rise, feed, and seek you. I thought, if I could figure out where he put you, then I could be there when you woke. You wouldn't have to be alone. We all looked. Eventually, the others decided we should wait to feel you when you woke. I couldn't. I had to know where you were, but I failed anyway. Ace's father told us you would rise, or I would've died when you did. Somehow. I can't be without you, Maci. I've known it since my own rising."

I sighed because thinking of my earliest memories wasn't comfortable. For him, I'd try. "It was dark. Cold. Dirty." I lifted one of my hands to look at my clean, even fingernails. "There were bodies everywhere. I shoved them aside as I pulled myself out of the earth. It took a long time because I had to rest often."

"We felt you rise. All of us did, like a pulse of light in the darkest night. We darted out, but it was imprecise, so I couldn't find you. Then you were moving. I think? If I had to guess, you were in the pit, wherever you awoke, for two risings."

That would make sense. I shivered. "I didn't know how much time, just that it took a long time. I was so hungry, and there was nothing to do but dig, climb, and push bodies." I'd rather never think of that time again, I realized with a shudder. "No more of this."

His lips brushed mine, and they felt warm and alive and nothing like the bodies in the dirt. "I think of it as the second time I failed you. I just needed to know how bad the failure was."

I lifted an eyebrow, wishing he would kiss me again instead of talking. "So that you can keep some sort of running tab of how much you owe me?"

"Yes. Exactly."

I groaned. "It would be better if you kissed me."

Caesar pulled us both up to sit, and I swatted at him. "What are you doing?"

"Feed," he said as he tilted his neck. "Come on, finish. You're hungry."

I was, there was no doubt about that. But I was always hungry, and there were things I wanted to say, so I said, "I don't like you feeding from humans. Not any of you. I fucking hate it."

He lifted an eyebrow. "You should still be too much in a haze to notice any of it, and yet you're incredibly cognizant, more and more so every day. You shouldn't be able to care enough to notice who we feed from, but I get it. I wouldn't want you feeding from anyone other than us, either. For now, though, while your need for food is still so extreme, we don't have a choice. There will come a time when we can feed solely from each other, because none of us will need to do it every day. For now, that's just not possible."

"Fuck you for being reasonable," I growled, then I threw him down beneath me. A second later, I bit back down right where I had earlier. I fed deeply. *If this is how it has to be, then so be it.*

Caesar moaned, the same sound he'd made when he was buried deep inside of me. I shivered with desire, a pulse of remembered pleasure making me rock against him. I reached for his cock as I sucked, and I stroked him. He shuddered, and I closed my eyes. We would both get what we needed.

He came in my hand about a second before I finished feeding from him. I lifted my head to find the beautiful man completely unconscious.

Sitting back, I sighed. I had to stop feeding before they conked out. It would be nice to have more conversations similar to the one Caesar and I shared.

Okay, it turns out I'm a talker. Who could have guessed?

I stood up, the remains of our fun dripping down my leg. *Whoops.* It looked like I needed another shower. At least I was starting to remember personal hygiene again. I made my way into the bathroom then stepped under the steaming water. It was instantly warm. Was that usual for showers? I didn't think so.

The door to the bathroom flung open, and I peeked around the shower curtain to see Rowan in the doorway. "Tanner and Caesar should never have left you by yourself."

I shrugged then let the hot water run down my body. I loved this feeling. *Did I used to scald myself under the spray when I was human?* "Caesar got drained and Tanner did, too, but he's up and feeding."

I heard the footsteps as Rowan strolled the rest of the way into the bathroom. "We're supposed to be making sure you are watched."

I pulled back the curtain again despite the water that flowed past me and onto the floor. "I'm a vampire, Rowan. I think I could defend myself from most things. Just not fire, apparently."

"There are many things you're not equipped to handle, although you soon will be, no doubt." He stepped closer, his gaze concerned. "Your father is very worked up."

"Well, it's not a picnic for me, either, so he can wait his turn."

My statement earned me a smile from Rowan. I had a feeling those weren't given out all the time, and a flush of heat warmed my cheeks with pleasure. He sighed and then stepped into the shower and under the water with me, fully dressed. I smirked at him. "You're going to get your pretty clothes wet."

"I couldn't care less." He tilted my neck back. "When you let someone bite you, it's submitting to them. I can't let that happen except with us. No one gets to bite you but us. Never."

I lifted an eyebrow but didn't wrench my neck away. Rowan could bite me if he wanted. In fact, I'd love it. I reached around him to grab the body wash then squeezed out a dollop of sweet-smelling soap into my hand. As he held me, I washed my pussy with the soap. He watched my hands, not letting go of my neck.

"What did you see today?" His words, seemingly so disinterested, contrasted the way he watched me and the bulge growing in his wet pants.

I didn't pretend to misunderstand him. "I saw all of them not listening to her, which meant that they all died."

"I suppose the lesson there is that we need to do a better job of listening to you." He bent over to kiss at my neck, his lips and breath warm against my already hot flesh. "I want to feed from you more than anything, but I don't want you to keep having to travel through memories."

I shook my head. "I'd have to feed from you, too, for it to work."

He kissed me again. "If you keep cleaning yourself like that, I'm going to come in my pants."

I hadn't even been thinking about it since I'd started doing it. Certainly, I hadn't been touching myself enough to elicit any kind of real pleasurable response. "Would you like to do that for me, Rowan? Then you can drink my blood, I'll drink yours, and we'll see what it is that we see together?"

"One thing at a time." He dropped his hand from my neck but only so he could push me against the wall by my shoulders. Rowan pressed a finger inside of me. "I think you're clean now, Maci. I wish you could remember what I remember. I know you will, but I have spent the better part of the last few years either wishing I could do this to you, remembering how we briefly did it, or remembering how it felt to sink into your heat. At this point, you might say I'm obsessed with you."

I spread my legs slightly to give him better access. He used the space to find and press against my clit, so I moaned. Pleasure surged through me, a resonating ripple of bliss. I closed my eyes. *Yes, I want more than that. So much more.* He found a rhythm I liked and he kept to it as I rocked my hips into his palm. I opened my eyes to watch him as he pleasured me. *Yes.* With eye contact, it was so much better. I caught my breath, my muscles starting to clench from his ministrations. *More.* This time I might have spoken the word aloud, but I wasn't sure. *What is even happening between us?* It didn't matter. But it did because I could feel something profound growing between us. The water, the quiet, his hand as it massaged my clit until my knees buckled. I exploded around him, my head hitting his shoulder until he supported my entire weight as I shuddered against him.

"Maci." He was hard, but he made no move to do anything about it, instead, stroking his hands down my skin in long, soothing strokes. I should do something with his cock. I wanted to. Badly. I just couldn't seem to bring myself to move right then. "I am so tired of you having pain. When you were a human, things were so hard for you. We can blame your father for that, since he put you in an untenable situation and left you to deal with it like you were nothing more than a board piece in a game to be played. It didn't get better when you were under our care, sadly. You died. Now, here you are, and you have to keep traveling back to some other life that wasn't even your own."

I managed to lift my head to meet his gorgeous eyes. "I think I'm strong. I think I was born in both lives to be that way. I don't think I break easily. Frederick had to burn her alive, that person whose memory I carry. It was the only way he could stop her. I don't think you have to be worried about me being in pain. I think I can conquer it time and again."

He kissed my forehead. "But you shouldn't have to. You captured our souls when we were just humans. We didn't understand then, but I do now. We're just souls when it comes down to it, and our souls love your soul. When you're done with this transition, I'm hoping you'll remember that."

I put my arms around his neck then tilted my head as a pounding started in my brain that I couldn't possibly ignore. "Speaking of pain…"

"What's wrong?"

I wasn't sure. It felt as if pressure built up in my head and wanted to rush out, wanted to force me to pay attention. Rowan reached around me to turn off the water. It was quiet, we were both wet, and in that second the pain exploded. My head felt like it was under water while the rest of my body remained in a frozen block of ice. I couldn't move, couldn't save myself from drowning, couldn't even scream.

Rowan tugged me against him even tighter. "What's wrong?" he repeated.

If I could have spoken, I would have told him. Despite the blinding pain, and in the midst of the most painful moment of my vampire life, I could suddenly remember her.

The human-Maci, the one who died so I could be born.

I gasped for air, wondering if I'd ever breathe properly again.

"I've got you. We'll get through whatever it is." He offered his neck to me. "Feed. Whatever it is, the blood will help."

Right then I couldn't, not while I was frozen in the block of ice. All that existed was memory.

And this time, at least, it was mine.

"You haven't spoken a word in hours." Ace ran a hand through my hair. "We can't help you if you don't tell us what happened."

I tilted my head to regard him. They all wanted an explanation I didn't feel like giving yet. I swallowed. I would need to feed again, but I doubted they'd feed me if I didn't explain. There was no way they would let the sunrise come without me telling them something.

"I can remember her," I finally said.

Tanner nodded. "Yes, we know. Griffin and Caesar traveled with you, remember?"

Did he think I lost my mind? I scowled at him then said, "Not those memories. Those belong to someone else. I'm not even sure why we have to carry them, other than to reiterate we may be truly fucked going forward. No, *my* memories. Maci's memories. The human version of me."

Caesar leaned forward, steepling his fingers as his brow cocked. "Really? So fast, I thought it took females months or years."

"Well, I think it's fair to say our Maci is rather exceptional." Ace sighed. "And maybe it's a good thing. You should know the whole history of who you are. Or were. How does it feel?"

"She froze in the shower like she was turned to stone and couldn't move." Rowan stared out the window. He didn't turn to face us, which would have intimidated my human-self. Not me. Human-Maci thought he was mean, cold, distant. By contrast, I could see he burned so hot, he had no choice but to shut it all down around him. Rowan went still for the benefit of other people, not for himself.

Ace pretended to feel more human than he did, hence him touching my hair the way humans did. Caesar didn't pretend anything, always entirely in the moment just as he was. Tanner never missed a thing, and Griffin was constantly lost in his own head, trying to solve problems. The human version of Maci only understood part of them.

But she had loved them, and they didn't love her—not in the way she could understand it anyway.

I wasn't going to answer Ace's question, since he didn't really care how I felt about having my memories back. He'd humor me, and the rest of them would stand by while he did. I was obviously fine. They weren't going to want more information than that. No, what Ace actually wanted to know had probably bashed at his vampire brain until he could hardly function from needing answers. So I answered those questions instead, the ones I knew he wanted to know but wouldn't ask.

"There wasn't anything you could have done to save her. Frederick meant for her to die. He always wondered if Maci would carry the memories he didn't want her to have. Once he became aware of her existence, that was that. It was delayed, but it was always going to happen. You should never have been able to stay awake in the daytime like that at all, and she didn't die blaming you."

He bent forward as if I struck him, and then he closed his eyes. "She should have."

"I'll say again, you shouldn't have even been awake. There was no way that you could save her from much more advanced and capable vampires just based on their age alone. I mean...it's honestly remarkable that you were awake at all." I shrugged. "Besides, if she didn't die, I wouldn't be here."

That, of course, begged a question. "Would you rather have her? Your human that you all adopted as your own? Or would you rather the vampire she was always meant to be?"

I didn't know exactly what I'd do if they said they wanted the human version of me. We didn't lie as vampires. It meant I needed to learn what questions to ask and what was better left unspoken.

Maybe. Or maybe we'd fight all the time because I couldn't keep my mouth shut. I already accepted that fact about myself.

"No." Ace shook his head. "How could you even suggest that? The second we found out you were coming, we've wanted nothing but you here. I don't know about the rest of them, but I'm blown away by you. I don't place much value on prophecies. Why bother? But I can see why they were afraid of having you back. Why they thought that, if they could control it, then they could stop what's going to happen."

I swallowed. "What *is* going to happen?"

"You're going to destroy them."

I closed my eyes. That sounded exhausting. "I don't know if I have it in me."

"You do." Tanner rose and crossed to me. "It's just too close to sunrise to contemplate right now. Come on. Time to lie down."

It was an idea I could get behind, but I had something else to say. "I don't want you guys feeding from humans anymore. Surely if I could handle your needs when I was human, I can do it now. I don't want you to eat from any more humans or I might kill them. All of them."

Caesar met Griffin's gaze before they both looked toward Rowan who still hadn't turned around. Their leader wasn't answering them. "Is there a problem, fearless leader, or are you just not talking anymore?"

"Something's wrong," he finally said, still looking out the window. "I've been feeling it all night."

Tanner frowned while Caesar and Ace jumped to their feet to join him. Griffin looked between us all. "It's not night anymore. It's practically daytime."

"They're day walkers, or most of them are. I'm not sure they'll stay away from us just because it's daytime, not if they know she's here." Rowan shook his head. "I can stay up awhile. We know Ace can."

Caesar sighed. "I can't. It's already pulling me under. Fuck."

"Me too." Griffin frowned. "And I don't understand how you two can stay awake. Tanner?"

"I'm not being taken under right this second, but that doesn't mean I won't be suddenly. I haven't tested it. I go to bed at sunrise. It just feels like the right thing to do."

I got to my feet. "I'm not the least bit tired."

I'd been exhausted moments earlier, but I found an unexpected surge of energy. "If someone is coming here, then I'll be ready."

"They're not.' Rowan walked over to me. "Not this morning, but *something* is coming. I can feel it on the back of my neck, like it's crawling toward us. I've always had these kinds of senses, ever since I was reborn. They know you're alive, and they're coming."

I didn't know much yet, but I was sure I didn't want to be burned alive. *Not again.* "I need to know how to battle."

"There are a few things we can show you." Caesar placed a hand on my back. His movements were sluggish. "But most of it will be instinctual."

I hoped he was right, because I didn't want to be killed before I even lived in this body. "She had a pointless life."

I didn't know I'd spoken aloud until they all stared at me with such stillness, it might have sliced through the room.

"I hope she didn't feel that way," Griffin said in a low voice. "She was absolutely pivotal to us in human and vampire life. There was so much about her that was important. When I look back at my human life, I feel like he was that way, too, but I think that might just be how we feel about the time before we become vampires. Perhaps it's natural to feel the fruitlessness of a non-vampire life as not having a point, but it did. I don't think we start from nothing as vampires. I think who they were shapes who we become greatly."

Was he right? Did that girl—the one who spent too much time just trying to survive—help to make me who I was somehow? "I want to speak to my father tomorrow," I said. I had questions for him.

"If we aren't attacked immediately upon waking, I'll take you to see him myself. As for the feeding request, yes, okay.

We'll try it. If it doesn't destroy you too much to feed all of us, then that's what we'll do. I don't want to touch a human when you're around anyway, I can assure you of that." Rowan shrugged. "And I don't need to be the leader if one of you would like to take the wheel. Until then, I suggest Ace and I stay up past sunrise to get used to it. The rest of you, get some sleep."

Tanner crossed to the windows and started to close the blinds. I blinked then shook my head. He really shouldn't be doing it alone, so I crossed to help him, and he smiled at me. His monster was always close, and mine liked that so much.

"How did you find out I was coming back?" I hadn't realized how much I wanted to know the answer until I asked. "Did you know I was dead before you found out or after?"

He visibly swallowed. "A few minutes afterward. We were told you were dead by Ace and his father—but that you'd be coming back. Frederick called to taunt Rowan about it, in fact. We...reacted badly. We intended to go out in a blaze of glory, so to speak, while we waited for you to rise, not that I could contribute to the plan. I can't talk without you, but I was happy to go along. Ace's father became more and more frantic. He had to run before he was caught. Quickly, he filled us in about you rising at some point and where we should go to wait for you—here, with your father. We haven't seen him since. Truthfully, we have no idea what happened to him. If your father knows, he's not telling us."

It was a mystery. How was Ace's father connected to mine? And Wanda, the woman who saved me when I was human–she was connected to Ace's father also, but I never saw her again after she made sure I was okay. Was she involved in this, too? I helped him close all the windows to keep the sun out while I contemplated the issues.

When I turned back around, Caesar was asleep sitting

up on the couch. Tanner grinned at me. "He can't stay awake at all when it's time to sleep."

It was sort of cute. I smiled at him. Was that a vampire thought? It seemed a lot like something my human-self would have found amusing. I walked over to Caesar and laid him down so at least he would be more comfortable.

Tanner leaned over to kiss me on the cheek. "I never wanted to be a vampire when I was human. I didn't love it when I woke up and couldn't talk, but now that you're here with us, part of us, among us, it's so much better. I think they know that. I think they understand there is something about you that will cause them problems. That's why they hate you and want you dead. We won't let them kill you again. They made us to fight their wars, and now they're going to get one the likes of which they couldn't possibly have imagined."

I kissed him back, right on the lips. "Maybe. But don't forget, it's really always about power. They're not afraid of me because I make things better. They're afraid of me because they're afraid I'll prove they really never had any to begin with."

9

I couldn't sleep. It was strange. As a vampire, I never experienced sleeplessness before. Insomnia was more of a human problem. Tanner was out cold next to me on the bed, and Griffin was across the room. I left an unconscious Caesar on the couch, but I could hear footsteps moving around in the living room area.

Ace and Rowan.

They were staying up, as promised. Rowan's ability to stay awake during the daytime must have been a newish thing since he wasn't able to ignore sleep when I was human. I rose from the bed and headed to the living room. Ace wasn't anywhere to be seen, but Rowan sat on a loveseat near Caesar. His head was in his hands, and he didn't look up when I came out.

Okay, he could be awake, but it wasn't going well for him. I didn't have any pain at all. I wondered why, but it was just another question to add to my ever-growing tally. I walked over to him and bent down to put my hands over his.

He jumped, like he had no idea I was there. Rowan's eyes were red, bloodshot. He was all vampire in that moment.

Even non-believing humans would change their minds if they could see him right then.

"How are you awake?" he asked, and his voice was low.

"Can't sleep, but you should. I know you're pushing through, but it's not good for you. You won't be able to help any of us in a fight like this."

Rowan furrowed his brow. "I agree, but I can't sleep. It's like I pushed too far."

"Come on." I took his hand and drew him from the chair. It was doubtful he could have stopped me if he'd wanted to right then.

I drew him back to the bed where I tried to unsuccessfully sleep before. He lay down next to me, but his eyes didn't close. If anything, the act of moving around made him seem even more in pain. I lifted my neck. "Feed."

"I'm not particularly hungry."

We'd been through the same song and dance when I was human, as if he had blinders on when it came to what he needed. Rowan looked out for everyone else but himself. "Feed yourself to sleep. You know it'll work. You'll even like it."

He sighed. "I don't want to take blood from you yet. Despite whatever miraculous abilities you may have, you're still a recently awakened vampire. A female vampire, at that, which is almost unheard of these days. I want to cherish and protect you until you're one hundred percent ready."

It was a sweet thought, but also not okay considering the circumstances. He would have to take blood from me one way or another if we ever wanted to recover the memories from the dead vampires.

"Rowan," I said as I drew his mouth toward my neck. "You need this, and I'll be fine. You won't take too much." I wasn't sure he could, even if he wanted to. "I was made to feed you even when I was human."

He ran his hand down the side of my body, stopping at my hip. "You're so beautiful. In every version of my existence, you fill me up inside, make me more than I was supposed to be. I would stay awake forever to keep you safe."

We were both sounding less our vampire selves and more like the humans we used to be. "Sweet sentiments, but I need you strong, and I'm not weak anymore, so let's be strong together. Feed. Sleep."

He shuddered against me. "I get hard when I feed from you."

That I knew, but he continued. "I like it. A lot."

"Okay." I lifted my neck again. "You're rambling."

He bit down, a low moan rumbling from his throat when he did. I was between him and Tanner on the bed, and it made a warm and comfortable cocoon to be between their two bodies. I expected Rowan to conk out almost immediately upon biting me, but he didn't. His body hardened against mine, and for long moments he drank down my blood. I ran my hand up and down his back, keeping him close to me. His pain moved through me. As human-Maci, I'd been acutely aware when they weren't okay, but the sense of their needs basically eluded me since I'd reawakened. I could feel it then, in the early light of morning. Slowly, his body softened, loosening as he fed, until his hand slipped off my hip, falling gently on the bed.

Rowan was out. Small breaths touched my skin where he'd been feeding as my blood dripped slowly down my neck. I pulled his mouth from where he'd latched onto me, his teeth receding from their fang state as he slept. I'd stop bleeding eventually, and my human propensity to not like mess wasn't with me anymore. *Let the blood drip until it stops on its own.*

Ace watched from the doorway. "He so wants to be able to do daytime for all of us, particularly for you. Yet here you are, awake, like it's not a big deal when just hours ago you were going to fall over."

I sat up, shrugging as I did. "That was before I realized we could be attacked during the day. Maybe it's what the humans call adrenaline?"

"Adrenaline doesn't make a difference for most of us. You think Caesar isn't loaded with that, thinking of you at risk? Tanner? They couldn't wake up if their life depended on it right now." Ace surged forward. "And it's still not exactly easy for me, although it's better than when you were killed. That was the kick in the ass to get better at being awake. I needed to be stronger."

He acted as if it was a choice he'd made, not something he battled against. "So maybe it just depends on the vampire?" I scooted off the bed. "You and I can react to adrenaline and circumstances, but for the others, it's just going to take time."

Ace's eyes trailed the dripping blood down my neck. After a moment, I lifted an eyebrow. "Want a bite, so to speak?"

His eyes flared red. "You know I do, but I'm not going to be okay with just a bite, and I'm supposed to be staying up to guard you."

I shoved gently at his chest. "I can guard myself. That's one of the beautiful things about going through this process. I'm not weak anymore."

He smirked at me. "There is being strong and then is being me. Do you remember my power from when you were human? I'm tougher than the rest of them, even if they'd never admit it."

"Oh, the ego." I shook my head. "Same in human men as vampires. I take that back; maybe you're worse." I slid my hand up his shirt and yanked him to me. "Take the blood. You want it, and I want you to drink from me."

He licked my neck—everywhere *but* the bleeding part. *Fuck, he is being such a tease.*

"I won't fail you. When you know that, I'll feed from you. Not before," he promised.

His alpha-male tendencies were hot, but they did nothing for me right then. I sighed, as if I surrendered to his will, but instead, I grabbed his neck. "If you won't feed, I will."

He nodded, drawing me even closer. "Please feed. Please do."

I bit down on his neck, drinking his blood down into me. He was warm, cinnamon-y and strong. It didn't take long until I was full, so I licked his wound closed as he shuddered against me. Ace really liked it when I fed from him.

"You can't be finished." Was that a plea I heard as much as a statement? He wanted me to keep feeding.

I ignored his question. "Do you know how you feel right now? How you're aching for my mouth on your body? That's how I feel right now. I'm not trying to be cruel. I'm actually full—but you are trying to be cruel, I think."

Ace made a sound that was more like a growl than a groan before he spoke against my ear. "I never want to leave you lacking, Maci, even if you're being a manipulative vampire right now. Congratulations, by the way. You fit right in."

He bit down on my neck. I knew we would both travel into other people's memories, yet still, the jerk backward took me by surprise. It was rougher than my first walk through her memories, and that had only been so painful because I hadn't known it was coming.

Then again, this was Ace. Everything with him was always a little rougher. It just seemed to be how he was made.

I sighed and looked around the memory landscape. The version of him from this reality stared back at me. "He left here in a fury. What did Frederick want from you?" He closed our front door and walked over to take my hands. "You look...shaky."

I supposed that was a good word for how I felt. The body I currently inhabited burned with a fury not my own but intense just the same. "He wanted me."

"Wanted you to do what?" He tapped my chin and grinned at me. "Everyone wants something from you. It's the nature of you being our fearless leader."

He didn't understand, and I couldn't blame him. In one hundred years, no one had ever tried to insert himself into my life the way Frederick just had. "He wanted me, darling. He wanted to have sex with me. He wanted me to leave all of you and be with him. When I declined his *gracious* offer, he attempted to get violent with me."

"Where did he just go?"

Ace's mouth fell open the second I began, and when he answered me, his vampire was in his voice. If I let him, he'd go full on eruption and drain Frederick's blood along with every young vampire in the next two counties. I couldn't blame him, since I'd do the same if someone touched him without his consent.

I grabbed his arm, pressing my fingertips hard into his skin to ensure he heard me. "He's not stable. I think he may have to be put down. He couldn't have thought my response would be any different. I'm in committed soul- mate relationships."

"He's out there telling people we need to change the way we do things. To control women. To use them for one thing and one thing only, which is breeding. He wants to make a mockery of everything we've always represented."

I blinked, remembering the present. So far, I moved through time in my memories of these people. I started with her death, and it seemed I traveled chronologically backward. They were just discovering what they already knew in the previous memories–that Frederick was fucked up. I knew it in my real life, too, considering he'd killed me.

I owed him payback for that poor human girl, the one I had been who felt both far away and close to me at the same time.

"He isn't going to live to see another day," the not-Ace man promised.

She patted him on the arm. "I don't know that it's worth it."

Boy, was she wrong. I caught my breath just in time to be thrust back into my own body and timeline. Blood still dripped down my neck and Ace bent over to lick it. I shuddered, his touch giving me a shiver of pleasure while being almost too much in my sensitized state. "Well, that sucked, but your tongue is heaven," I admitted aloud.

He made a sound that might have been an affirmation or might have just been a grunt because he wanted to feed from me some more. I offered him more of my throat, and he bit down hard. I closed my eyes. Yes, it felt fantastic. My body trembled with need, my hands skimming his body impatiently. I wanted Ace to take more, to get what he needed from me.

We were both awake. These moments belonged just to us, which made them more precious somehow.

He yanked away from me, licking the remainder of my blood from his lip with a quick swipe of his clever tongue. Ace winked at me before his face fell.

What was wrong? I looked around as a noise caught my attention. It was the slightest buzzing, but it was getting louder.

This was a new phenomenon since I'd woken up a vampire. "What is that noise?"

"Danger. Not all of us can sense it, but seems you can. I have it, too. There are people coming to hurt us, kill us." He backed up and looked around. "We have to protect them. No, scratch that. I have to protect all of you."

I grabbed his arm. "We're the only ones awake. I'm strong, okay? I woke up a vampire. I'm like you. That woman I keep seeing, they hurt her. A lot. That's not me. I have no intention of dying like that. I'm fighting with you, Ace, by your side. If this is what we think it is—all of us together—then I'm here with you."

He wanted to argue, I could see it in the glare in his eyes. Instead, he nodded. "Okay. You and I are up. We have to keep this house safe. Your father and others can daywalk. We need them to wake up. If they've already gone to sleep, they may not wake up. Otherwise, it's just you and me. Go house to house in this area. You can't get confused. There is nothing around us except your father's group. See who is up. In the meantime, I'll hold them off."

I frowned. "Can you do that alone?"

"I can. Don't forget how incredibly strong I am. There aren't that many of them. Maybe ten? I can manage."

I had to believe him. Much as I was sure that I could handle myself, I'd never battled before. Ace had—a lot. I had to trust him. He needed experienced vampires by his side, so I'd do my best to find them for him.

I ran out the front door. The smell of humans assaulted my nose, and I ignored the sense. I didn't want to feed from them. It didn't mean they weren't the equivalent of a cookie to my old human-self; they could be a snack, but I would control myself. There were more pressing things to do than drinking human blood.

My ears buzzed louder. They were getting close. Whoever Frederick sent to attack us. I knew Frederick would never come himself, not when he could send someone else to do it. He'd be too cowardly to do anything besides light a match and watch it burn.

I didn't know where my father lived versus the others, but I didn't need to worry. The doors started to fly open as I approached, and vampires I didn't know appeared on their doorsteps. Maybe they were all getting buzzed like me, or maybe some of them just told the others. It wasn't a huge crowd, maybe eight vampires, but I was glad to see them.

My father appeared before me. "They let you outside alone?"

I wasn't going to respond. It really wasn't the time. Instead, I nodded to him in greeting and asked, "Is anyone else up?"

"These are the daywalkers among us. Don't worry, daughter. They don't have more than we do. We will beat them back, and then we will move so they can't find us again."

We would run? That didn't sound right to me. What was the point? I didn't ask, though, because there was too much to do. When he would have left my side, he turned around instead. "Our family always has daywalkers. I'm not surprised you are one of them."

I wasn't his family, not really. I was just a girl he'd brought to life so that he could have the memories I carried with me. He didn't even raise the human-me himself. No, he left her with a drug addicted human who completely neglected her. He was lucky I was there at all.

But I'd save those words for when we weren't under attack.

I followed behind him, since he seemed to know where he was going. In the distance, I saw nothing but darkness. My nose twitched. The scent of the approaching vampires rode the wind, as if their ill intent for me carried an actual scent. It made me want to growl in the back of my throat. *Am I a vampire or a werewolf?* The thought made me smile.

Yanked backward abruptly, I knew it was Ace who had me before I could even see him. I recognized his scent. He was mine. I'd find him anywhere.

"I was hoping you'd stay back there a little longer."

I lifted an eyebrow, not that he could see it with my back pressed to his chest. "I didn't have to find them. They all heard the same signal we did."

He nodded and kissed the back of my neck. "That's wonderful."

Excitement moved through me, like a buzz of electricity. Only it wasn't my own. It was Ace's. "You're looking forward to this," I accused, tilting my head to try to see him behind me.

"We ran from them so we could be separate when you rose. I have pain to dish out to these fuckers," he admitted with a bloodthirsty grin.

And then they were there. A dozen daywalking vampires faced us, their fangs visible and all in battle mode. My vision tunneled. I'd never fought before, and so far, I didn't have any memories that included fighting from the visions I had from that other woman's life. Despite that, I felt absolutely confident I could battle just as well as the other vampires present. If I'd been in the mood to laugh, I would have, because it was as though the will to battle surged in my blood.

I launched forward alongside Ace, who took down a vampire who once fed on the human version of me. He'd hurt her, I remembered, so I was glad Ace was about to tear out his throat. I hoped his death hurt, and I hoped he died slowly from the assault, since no one would be around to close his wound and feed him blood.

I was sure that Ace could be counted on to take care of it.

As for me, I leaped onto the back of the nearest enemy and drove him to the ground. I recognized the vampire I pinned, also. He'd fed on her a lot—at least once a day, and he caused her pain and humiliation while he fed.

His eyes widened as he stared back at me. "You! How?"

I didn't know if his question was about how I was alive or how I was awake. Either way, I didn't care to answer. No, my job right then was to cause him pain before I killed him. I wasn't a woman who would be burned alive. I was one who would do the burning. Each and every one of them, if I had to, and if they begged me for mercy, they'd find I had none left to give.

"You're going to wish you'd never been changed," I promised him. I didn't know how I knew he wasn't a born vampire, but I did. They'd made him one of their own as a reward for something, but maybe my predecessor had known that.

I didn't care. He tried to roll me over, but I was tougher than him. I was young but I wasn't weak. I tore out his throat then roared with delight.

It couldn't be all there was to life, but if I had to endure war, then I was glad that there was pleasure to be taken from it. Damn it, I would not lose to these monsters. They would get out of *my* way this time.

I WAS COVERED in blood when I limped back toward our home. Ace was, too. The sun hung lower in the sky. We'd fought all day, and not slept at all. I'd been elated—thrilled, even—every second of the day, but with the fighting over, the lack of sleep started to weigh on me.

The twelve vampires who came for us were dead. None of us were. I smiled at that. I didn't know the names of any of the vampires who were with us except my father and Ace, yet I felt connected to them. We survived together.

"We'll get packed up to go," my father said to the group. "Before the end of the night."

I shook my head, wishing he'd just kept quiet. "That isn't the answer."

"We're not ready to take them all on," my father replied, exhaustion heavy in his tone. All of us looked more haggard, though, and ready to sleep.

"Seems like we did," Ace spoke up, squeezing my hand. "They know where we are, and we know where they are. We could come at them, too." He held up his hand. "Let's wait for Rowan. You're going to want to talk to him. Trust me."

My father stopped walking. "I'd like to talk to you two, since you were here today."

"He would have been, if such a thing were possible," I said through clenched teeth. "And I won't allow you to even attempt to create discord within my family. Whatever else we are, we are solid, is that clear? Ace wants you to wait for Rowan, so that's what you're going to do."

He sighed. "Daughter, you and I need to talk."

"Not now. We need to sleep. I'll speak to you in the next rising." I paused. "With Rowan."

He nodded, which was the best I would get under the circumstances. We turned toward the house that was, at least for the moment, ours. We might be running from it soon, I thought with a sigh. Doors opened and closed around us. Some of the older vampires who didn't daywalk but could rise relatively early stepped onto the porches.

The sun burned my skin as I stared at them, watching them as they stared back at me. I guessed I was a bit of a novelty, as the vampire they all waited for since my father set the whole mess in motion. *Whatever.* The sun didn't trouble me during battle, but it was now. I had to get inside.

One woman covered her mouth with her hand, and I could see tears in her eyes. She wasn't the one they'd called my mother, so I didn't know why she would be so worked up over seeing me.

"Ace?" Her voice was low. "I've waited..."

He stared at her. "You."

That told me nothing. I squeezed his hand. "Who is she?"

"My mother." He scrunched up his face. "How are you here? Frederick killed all the women."

"Your father saved me." She put out her hand. "I..."

He held up his to stop her. "I can't... Soon, okay? There's too much for this. Just too much. How long have you been here?"

Her chin quivered. "I was told to stay away from you. He told me to wait until things were settled."

Ace shot my father a look that could have burned him to the ground. As my human-self had once been held against a wall by the force of his power alone, I knew just how powerful his gaze could be. My father should consider himself lucky Ace wasn't as angry anymore as he once had been. Also, that he was tired as fuck right then.

"Come on." I tugged on his arm. "You can talk to her when I talk to him."

He nodded. "Sounds like a plan."

We absolutely didn't have a plan, but one was forming in my head. Soon, we'd have some answers.

10

"What the fuck?" Rowan leaped from his bed, staring at Ace and me as if we stepped in from another dimension. He must have just woken up. The others weren't stirring yet.

I looked down at my blood-soaked arms. My whole body was covered in sticky redness, but none of it was mine. Rowan wouldn't know that, so I grinned at him, my head hazing over a little bit. I'd never been drunk as a human, not once, but my exhaustion felt something like the descriptions I heard from others.

"I do look a little bit like a crime scene, don't I?"

Ace kissed my cheek, but he was as covered in blood as me. He explained, "We were attacked. Fought all day, but we won."

Rowan's mouth fell open. "What?"

I patted his arm. "We fought..."

"I heard him," he interrupted me. I was too warped in the head right that second to care. Instead, I walked past him and headed toward the bathroom. I would shower, get the blood off, and go to bed for as long as I could sleep. If I could at all. I didn't know how that worked in the middle of the night for vampires. Could we sleep when the night had fallen?

"Are you okay?" Rowan grabbed my arm. "Are you hurt? Do you need blood?"

I kissed his cheek. "Feeling a little bit drunk, but not injured."

"It's the lack of sleep." He cupped my cheek. "None of that is yours? I can't smell through it. My senses have gone haywire."

Ace leaned against the wall. "You should have seen her. She was fucking amazing. At first, I was nervous but not now. She's tough. Maybe even tougher than you."

"I'm getting a shower. You two can compare dick sizes while I do. I don't need the 'who is the strongest' thing you're heading toward."

Ace laughed but Rowan didn't. "Tell me what happened, Ace. Don't leave out a single detail."

I tuned them out as I walked into the bathroom and turned on the spray. Stepping under the water, I hummed to myself. Usually, being exhausted would be painful. I understood that in my gut. It was something all vampires knew. But I felt better than I ever had. Was it the adrenaline from the fight? Or was it because I managed to deal some revenge against people that hurt her?

The door opened and closed. I breathed in, and a familiar scent tickled my nose—Ace. "Can you share that water?" he asked.

I moved, and he joined me under the spray. The blood sluiced away from both of us, coating the floor of the shower before it rushed down the drain. Ace ran his hands through my hair, lathering shampoo into my locks as he did. I hadn't even noticed him grabbing the bottle. It was the drunk feeling, making me less than totally focused. I took the bottle from his hands and began to lather his body as he'd done mine.

"More?" he asked, and I had the good sense to know he wasn't talking about the shampoo.

I smiled. "Against the wall?"

"Yes, my love. Whatever you want, however you want it."

Ace took my directions really well, pushing me against the wall. We stared at each other. "Why did I like that so much?"

He nipped at my chin. "Because you're a vampire, Maci, and we can be civilized with the best of them, but sometimes we really want to be the monsters."

"Dish out pain to our enemies," I added before I kissed him roughly.

Ace didn't wait. He lifted me up, and before I could even think about it, he was inside of me. His cock drove all the way inside, balls deep, as I cried out. Pleasure and pain warred, just as I liked it. "Pin me," I whispered in his ear. "Like you did when I was a human. Or are you too tired?" My question was both a taunt and a legitimate concern. The two sides of me forever warred with each other.

I did love their shower. I closed my eyes and let him drive my back into the cool tiles on the wall. I moaned, each thrust sending a new cascade of shivers through my body. *Yes, I want more like that. So much more.* I dug my fingers into his back. Ace wouldn't break from the pain—in fact the noises he made in my ear told me just how much he liked it. A human would be frightened of him—she had been—but I wasn't. I loved his darkness, because it matched my own soul. Our monsters understood each other.

I saw it on the battlefield when he looked up at me, drenched in a coat of blood. We matched. As he fucked me into the wall so hard we might break it, I couldn't help but grin at the thought.

"Hey," he said, then tugged on my hair, turning my face toward him so our eyes met. "Here, with me."

I nodded, lifting my neck to offer it. If he wanted to feed while he was buried deep inside me, he was more than welcome. But he shook his head once. No, Ace didn't want my blood. He only wanted my pleasure. I understood him, because I wanted the same thing for him.

I squeezed myself tighter around him until he pumped harder. *Harder. And more.* I could hardly think. I ran my hands down his chest, feeling his strong muscles bunch under my touch. Ace exuded power, and it was sexy as hell. The spiral of tension built within me, climbing ever higher as we gasped out our shared pleasure. Finally, and all too soon, I cried out, coming around him again and again.

He wasn't done, and I loved the feel of him finishing inside of me while I quaked in tremors from the high he gave me. I leaned my head on his shoulder. "Wasn't sure if I could sleep at night," I said with a jaw popping yawn.

Ace kissed my cheek. "I think tonight we both can."

"Okay." That sounded just fine to me. I snuggled closer to him, enjoying the feel of his warmth and the cool sheets.

"I'm sorry I got your human-self killed. I'll always be sorry, but I'm very glad you're here as you are, Maci."

I kissed his shoulder with my eyes still closed. "You didn't get her killed. But we *are* going to kill the fucker who killed her."

I really couldn't remember if I said anything else because sleep stole me away.

〜

I ONLY SLEPT A FEW HOURS—OR that's what it felt like—curled against Ace, who was still next to me, when the bed dipped. My eyes were heavy but I forced them open. Tanner stared at me, but it wasn't the Tanner I knew. His monster regarded me from his quiet gaze, but it wasn't anger I saw there or the need to feed. No, he was worried.

I sat up and stroked the side of his face, blinking hard to try to focus my eyes. "You okay?"

He scooted closer to me. I could sense Caesar pacing around in the hallway like I was out there with him. Griffin slammed a book down across the house. Rowan wasn't inside. He'd gone somewhere. It was harder to get a read on him. Ace was out cold, as if daylight had pulled him under. But much as I'd passed out hard, I was surprisingly awake now.

I got onto my knees. "You don't like that you slept through the battle?"

He couldn't talk to me, but I could understand Tanner just fine. We always managed to speak the same language without using words. Even when she'd been human, and I hadn't been there yet, we understood him.

I explained. "It isn't your fault. Some vampires can't rise during the day ever. You're still newly made. I don't know why I can, but I'm sure someday you will. They knew that. That's why they came when they did. It's a good thing Ace and I are weird. You'll get there. That's all. We fought to keep all of you safe."

I might as well have struck him. Tanner's expression said he didn't like it at all. I frowned. "It's not your job to keep me safe. It's our job to keep *each other* safe. You'll take care of me, and I'll take care of you. I'm not going to argue about that, either." I grinned at him, and he rolled his eyes at me.

"I'm pretty kick ass, Tanner. I kept up with Ace. They didn't get to me, not once."

He tilted his neck. Okay. He had something to say, and I couldn't blame him for that. Much as I could understand him, it still had to be frustrating for him. I bit his neck and shuddered with pleasure as the warm essence of Tanner filled me. I usually only took a little bit from him because he needed his voice but suddenly I was starving, and not for just any blood. I really needed *his*.

I crawled onto his lap and drank until I was full. After closing his wound, I lifted my head. Had I taken too much? No, his eyes were clear. He was still fine.

"Don't get cocky, Maci. They sent vampires that died. Next time, they'll send better ones."

I licked my lips because I liked how he watched me do it. "Maybe we'll take the fight to them?"

Tanner smoothed my hair off my forehead. "Not until we've all memory traveled. Only me and Rowan left, right? I think it's important or you couldn't do it. Frederick wanted us without you for some reason..."

I put my hand on his arm. "Because he tried to rape her. Maybe he doesn't want me to remember that and tell others."

Tanner growled, his monster tearing through his gaze. He'd burn the frickin' world for me.

I shook my head, stroking his arm. "It wasn't me. It was her. In this persona of me, I've never dealt with Frederick. I know what he did to her. He killed her. Tried to rape her. Hurt her. Took from her. I know that he killed the human that was me, but I'm okay. I don't intend to let him get anywhere near me again. Third time will be the charm."

He blinked, some of his anger lessening. "I like that idea. Let's do the time travel, then I'll let you rest again. If Caesar knew I was in here, he'd kill me. I was supposed to be letting you sleep. He's in a rage because you were in danger without him. We all are, but Caesar is losing his shit. The rest of us are just quieter."

I lifted an eyebrow. "How did you get in here, then?"

He smiled. "I'm the trickiest of all of us. No one realizes it, but I am. He turned to look at a noise I caused, and I walked right inside." Tanner shrugged. "At some point, he'll cue into the fact that I'm in here, so let's do this before I have to wrestle him to stay with you."

I'd seen such bad stories from this woman's life. The last thing I wanted was more of that, but I'd agreed to it, and at this point it was like the humans ripping off a bandage. I just needed to get it the heck done.

I turned my neck. "Bite away."

Tanner nodded. "I look forward to the day we can just leisurely lie in bed. We'll both wake up together, and I'll just roll over or you will. We can feed at the same time, with nothing to do but start the day like that."

Actually, it sounded like heaven. "Is that possible?"

"Someday." He nodded. "I'm sure of it."

I hoped he was right. "I had an incredible time battling. I felt better afterward than I have since I woke up a vampire. Still, I don't think I could do it every day. I think I might go mad. Lose my mind. Be a shell of what I'm supposed to be."

I was basically incoherent to rational thought until Tanner woke me up. The thought worried me. I didn't want to be more monster than woman. I needed to be both.

"I won't let that happen," he promised, his voice low. Ace still slept next to us despite the fact we weren't quiet. Tanner laid me back down then cuddled up to my other side, sandwiching me between him and Ace. He breathed me in for a long second and the sound moved through me. Ace must have dressed me, because I wore a nightgown and undies. The latter were instantly soaked. Would there ever be a time when I wasn't wet and ready for these guys? I hoped not.

He bit down on my neck gently. Tanner was the most tender of all of them, taking such care with me—which was funny, since his monster shimmered the closest to the surface. He could be violent, yet he never was around me.

I sighed as pleasure flooded me a second before I landed back in the memories of a woman I'd never know but who I spent a lot of time with lately, despite never having met her. I literally ran around in her mind, and she had apparently been lodged somewhere in mine the whole time. Did she influence my human-self in some ways? I'd never know for sure, but it was interesting to think about.

She laughed, distracting me from my wandering thoughts. I watched through her eyes as she touched her version of Tanner. "Read it again," she asked him.

He dropped the book he held. "I won't do it if you're going to laugh at me."

I smiled. "Oh, come on. You love it when I tease you." She got on her knees and crawled to his side then snuggled against him. "I love it when you do all the voices."

"I'm sure the Bard himself would have been thrilled with my performance voices. He'd hire me on the spot."

I rolled over to stare at his handsome face. "Do you think he was a vampire?"

He shook his head. "Not that I've ever heard," he replied as he touched the end of my nose. "I think about writing."

"You should." He smiled at me. When he looked at me like that, it did funny things to my insides. It was so easy to love him.

He leaned on his elbow, playing with a strand of my hair. "You make everything better."

I blinked and I was back in my body. The memory seemed so different from the others. For one thing, it hadn't featured Frederick. It also wasn't dire. No, I simply remembered a quiet moment shared between the two of them. I smiled, realizing for the first time that there *had* been more to her life than just constant pain. She had fun while she was alive, found peaceful moments, and she loved. My smile faded as a pang hit my heart. She really lost quite a lot in the fire Frederick started. Her existence included joy. I might not have experienced much joy in this life or the last, but after experiencing it from her memories, I was willing to fight for it.

Tanner licked at my neck. "I won't lose you like he did." He shuddered and I stroked a gentle caress along the back of his neck. While I was only seeing moments, the rest of them saw the full picture, knew their entire lives.

"I have no intention of dying like that."

He nodded then continued to drink from me. The soft press of his lips, the gentle stroking of his tongue, his hands on me—all of it combined to be soothing, yet it lit up my body with alertness. I had to protect them as much as they did me, and I felt the push to do so like a visceral need. "Do you think that we like each other the way we do because of them?"

It felt like a reasonable question. Why else would we all have agreed to just fall into a relationship together instead of taking time to get to know each other, and time to decide?

He closed my wound then propped himself on an elbow to regard me. "No."

Well, that was a definitive answer. "Why not?"

"Because how he felt isn't how I feel. I mean, he seemed like a nice guy but also a bit of a dumbass."

I snorted and covered my mouth to stop another giggle

from escaping as he kept talking, albeit with a grin on his face because he mirrored my humor.

"I think what happened, Maci, is that we all fell for each other as humans. I think my human-self considered the guys as his friends. You were the girl he so wanted to love, it carried over into the now, into becoming a vampire. I loved the human you were when I was a vampire, and there was no question in my mind I'd love you now. I didn't know how cool you would be, how strong, or how you'd do things vampires shouldn't be able to do so quickly after waking. We should still be deep in the realm of you draining us dry every hour, not to mention you shouldn't be able to talk yet. But here you are..." His voice trailed off. "I bet if we ever see the whole prophecy—the one that is hidden away, the one that made them all rush to have children that carry the memories—we'd finally find out why he was so desperate to keep you away. I bet he knew you'd kick ass."

Tanner didn't talk much, but when he did, he said all the right things. I smoothed my finger down his nose. "I don't see everything you guys do."

"This is playing out the way it's supposed to, I'm sure of that." His monster echoed his certainty. I could feel it in the way I always could with him.

"Why, Tanner, you're a romantic!" I mocked, fanning myself just to see the dimple appear in his grin again. If every day could be like those fleeting moments, I would be glad to rise at sunset and never give anything but those moments my attention.

But I knew better than that. There were things to do. I rubbed my eyes, wishing I had time to rest or, hahaha, take a vacation. "Take me to see my father," I requested instead.

I was more than capable of going by myself, but I sensed he'd feel better if he escorted me. In fact, if Caesar's energy was any indication, I'd probably be bringing an entourage. I glanced over at Ace to find him still dead asleep. I kissed his cheek, and he didn't stir, so I decided to let him rest.

"How are you up when he's still so out of it?"

I shrugged. "You tell me. You've been a vampire longer than me, Tanner."

He shook his head. "Doesn't feel that way, gorgeous. More like I finally came alive when you were reborn."

Now that is something to think about.

CAESAR GRUMBLED the entire way over to my father's house. Apparently, Rowan was already there. Caesar filled me in through clenched teeth as he shot daggers at Tanner with his gaze. He didn't like that Tanner had woken me up.

I kissed Caesar's cheek, which cheered him up. Not enough for him to stop grumbling, but a little bit. Griffin remained quiet as he walked next to me, and we all followed Tanner. I was right—all of my vampires who were awake wanted to come to see my father, even though Rowan waited for me there.

Tanner stopped abruptly, and I almost plowed into his back. The reason for his sudden stop—it wasn't just Rowan waiting for us at my father's house. In fact, a whole circle of vampires stood with my dad. I recognized one of them from the fight, but the others were all new to me. They all turned to stare like monsters in a horror flick while we approached.

Rowan lifted a questioning eyebrow, but otherwise didn't comment on their presence. He held out his hand toward me, palm up. "Darling?" I recognized his invitation for me to join him, or at least I thought I was who he called. I've never heard him call Tanner *darling*.

I stepped around Tanner, although Caesar growled when I left his side.

"Out," my father said to the rest of the assembled vampires. The man I recognized but whose name I didn't know nodded at me. The rest stared at me as if I was a brand new and strange creature they'd never seen before.

I'd noticed they considered me a spectacle last night. I was apparently the new shiny object they all waited for and they couldn't believe they were finally seeing me in person.

I was dressed, but my interest in primping in front of a mirror for the meeting was zero. I just didn't do it.

Rowan tugged me against him. "She's here, so say what you wanted to say to her."

My father shook his head. "I have things to say, and they're not going like that, Rowan."

"I'd like to hear what you have to say. Shall we go inside?" I indicated his house.

He nodded. "Yes, let's go."

Rowan smirked at me. "You're so formal."

"I've been spending too much time in her head. I'm starting to pick up her language."

He sighed. "Guess that just leaves me?"

"Yes, we need you. Otherwise, we're all done."

His body stiffened. "Okay."

Apparently, Rowan wasn't looking forward to his time traveling experience with me. Maybe the others told him horror stories? I really didn't know at this point. They all died eventually in the memories, and at least I only remembered dying once. It wasn't an experience I was sure my mind could stand reliving for each of them, but I supposed remembering was better than not living through it.

I stepped into my father's home. If he thought my guys were going to leave me alone with him, he had another think coming. They remained so close behind me, if I stopped moving, they would've collided like a row of dominoes falling over. Their unspoken message came across clearly, though—they weren't being separated from me.

"Where is Ace?" My father scanned across the faces filling his living room.

I shrugged. I could tell he wasn't a fan of disrespect, and it was just irreverent enough to amuse me. "He had something to do," I answered vaguely.

My father didn't need to know Ace still slept. It might make him look vulnerable in some way. Of course, worrying about seeming vulnerable to them was lunacy. We all awoke with abilities far beyond the normal. Ace could stay awake during the day, which practically made him superhuman compared to other vampires.

But my father would still see weakness in us, I was sure of it. Whatever his motives were, he was part of Frederick's generation.

And none of them were to be trusted. Ever.

My temper was rising, and I knew I had to keep my cool, so I looked around his house to give myself time to breathe. It was decorated as though he'd lived there a long time. Framed art decorated his walls, varying from animals to abstract in nature. *I bet my human-self would have understood what the artwork meant. She was smart.*

I blinked. Toward the end of her life, she forgot about that, but she *had* been quite intelligent. Anger surged through my veins. The man in front of me, despite his eclectic taste in art, caused the shit that poor human girl didn't survive.

Screw calming my anger, I decided. "Talk," I snapped. I didn't particularly feel like being polite right then.

He sighed and gestured to his blue couch. "Would you like to sit?"

"Nope." I snapped off the end of the word with a puff of noise even I found slightly annoying.

Griffin threw himself down on the couch and grinned at me. No one invited him to sit, but he was going to anyway. I grinned back at him. Whatever circumstances made them all mine, I was so glad that they were. Sometimes irreverent, sometimes difficult, sometimes funny...they were so many things. And if we could survive Frederick—as I was determined we would—I'd have a lifetime to know them inside and out.

I was counting on us being wildly successful.

My father had information. *Enough is enough, already.* "All right, Dad. Talk." I crossed my arms over my chest. I was done waiting.

11

"After Frederick killed off all the elders..." He looked away for a second. "I was wracked with guilt."

That was interesting. Not his guilt per se—although, fine, good to know—but that Frederick had killed *all* the elders. Not just the ones whose memories we held, then. That choice made the guys who she thought of as the young ones the actual elders themselves, thereby determining what was and wasn't truth for the vampires. *There was no one left to contradict him.* I blinked and forced myself to concentrate.

He got to pick his truth.

My father sat down on the couch. "Things went badly very quickly. He killed off most of the females. The ones who survived went into hiding. Some of them are here. Eventually, they found their way to us, but most of them were lost. He *hated* women, and I have suspicions as to why. He loved one who didn't love him back. Someone maybe you know, Maci."

I wasn't going to deny it, but he was wrong all the same.

"That wasn't love. If you love someone, you'd never try to force them to do things physically with you that they don't want to do. That's *power*. He tried to exert his power over her, and he wasn't able to do it. I haven't seen all of her memories, but I can guess they beat the crap out of him for it. They probably humiliated him. Make no mistake, you can say what you will, but none of this was about love. His ego got crushed after he didn't get away with doing something atrocious."

We were monsters. We could kill to feed, yet even vampires had lines they didn't cross.

"True," my father agreed with a nod. "Before he killed them, he became obsessed with a prophecy regarding what basically sounded like vampire souls reincarnating. They come back, embedded with memories similar to what we've seen in some animals. Genetic memories, you could say. He thought he could have the best of the ones who passed without having to deal with the rest of it." He stared at me. "I was against the idea. I mean, you can't just go around messing with destiny and things like that. If people are meant to come back from the dead, sort of, then they'll do it on their own."

He held his hands out at the end, as if pleading for me to understand his position. My father was such a mixture of confidence and confusion. He still hadn't entirely made up his mind about where he stood on the events, yet he'd lived through them. They called him the betrayer. He'd clearly done something that had triggered the war we were now in. I was shocked so many chose to follow him. I'd much rather listen to Rowan or Ace, since he wasn't inspiring a huge amount of confidence in me.

Yet I'm alive because of him.

He continued speaking, enthusiastic now that he'd

gotten started. "I thought he was just spouting off at the mouth. I never trusted him, no, but he considered me a friend, and I let him. It seemed...safer. Anyone else who could have helped me was gone at that point. I hung around. I wasn't the only one uncomfortable with the situation. I asked about Ace earlier, because his father was also uneasy. We just kept to ourselves. Finally, after many years, Frederick adopted the policy of making humans our servants by telling them he'd make them vampires. Only he never changed the females. Ever. He hasn't made one single human female a vampire. Not one! The men, sure, if they were stupid. They stay easy to manipulate when they're reborn, and they become his lackeys." He sighed. "It was awful. He'd have the lackeys kill the human women and tell the female servants still working how they were being made into vampires. After a few people started to see through him, he decided it was time we had kids."

The guys stayed remarkably quiet while he spoke. I didn't know how much of the story they knew from their retrieved memories or the books they'd read. It certainly involved them currently as much as it did me. I sat down next to Griffin, sliding my hand onto his thigh. My refusal to sit to annoy my father was beginning to feel ridiculous. Caesar scooted over to sandwich me, but Rowan didn't move. He stood, arms crossed, and Tanner moved to stand behind me.

I was glad they were there. I knew I could fight—as I proved and then some—but their company made me more secure. My father proved a different kind of battle.

"So, then what did you do?"

He'd stopped talking. We weren't going to leave the story unfinished.

Frederick sighed. "They picked women. I'm told he acts

like it all just worked the first time we tried it. It didn't. I refused to participate, so they wrote me off as ridiculous. Even Ace's dad got into it at that point. They impregnated five different women, and they didn't produce the right babies. They had some girls. They were just vampire babies —not the ones he wanted—so he killed them. I don't know how many cycles of trials they did. He finally came up with the idea of using ultrasounds. If one of the babies was a girl, he slaughtered all five mothers, over and over. There had to be *five* boys, end of story. Anything else meant death to the mother."

Imagining them planning and then executing, literally, the plan—it was so horrific, I almost couldn't stand listening, but he continued. "And then the unthinkable happened. It actually *worked*. Five boy babies. There was a twist, too. Ace's dad fell in love with the woman he'd impregnated. He might have had some compunctions about what they did to begin with, and they finally blossomed into true horror when he saw what was being done, what he'd willingly participated in doing. It was like he came back to his senses. Right around that same time, I got really scared. Honestly, boys, I didn't want you back here without her. She made the five of them tolerable."

Griffin snorted. "That is probably still true, but I need you to understand—we aren't the six of them. We're ourselves. Yes, we have memories of a random person embedded in us and we have since we awoke. It's strange, but he doesn't influence me. I don't really care what he did, because he did everything all wrong."

"Maybe that's the point." Rowan shrugged. "To know what *not* to do."

"You haven't seen it yet." Tanner spoke low. "You'll feel differently. I mean, I'm glad to know just how bad Frederick and the others are. I really am, but I already knew. My human-self grew up with them. I would've killed them anyway just for that shit, not to mention the fact they killed Maci."

Rowan nodded. "I'm sure you're right."

I considered Rowan for a long second after he spoke. It must be exhausting, having to lead all of us and be questioned all the time. Although it seemed like a conversation we should have, it wasn't the right time. Some time, though, we'd sit down to discuss some Rowan self-care. Maybe he'd like to try to hunt me? I shoved those thoughts aside and asked, "What did you do when you decided you couldn't put up with it anymore?"

"Ace's Dad came to me first because he knew I'd made a decision. I intended to thwart their plans. I was going to have you, and I knew what steps to take to make it happen. I met your mother, but then...she changed things for me. She was everything. Together we had this place, and we had you."

He said it so nonchalantly, but I saw through him. "How many babies and their mothers did you have to get rid of to have me?"

My blunt question made him scowl. "None. You came right away, which is particularly amazing because your mother is a vampire. Vampire women statistically take longer to conceive than humans, which was why Frederick used them in the first place. But you came to us right away."

Gak, I did not want to think about my parents making me right then or ever, but then a memory hit me, or rather the feeling of one. My human-self dealt with a lot of things she found completely disgusting. I smiled at the sense of it, of her. It was the first time I thought of her and didn't really feel sadness or disappointment on her behalf.

Griffin put a hand on my knee. "As we all know, she didn't grow up with a vampire mother and father. You left her with a human to raise her. A bad human, at that."

He winced. "Yes, I chose poorly, I agree. But we needed someone who could be enthralled enough that they wouldn't notice if we took you periodically. We wanted someone who wouldn't care if you started living with one of your men. We expected it to happen a lot faster than it did, honestly. I was convinced they would bond with you as children, but it was like you all went out of your way to avoid her." The last was said to the guys, not me.

Rowan shook his head. "I can assure you, the human who once inhabited this body would have loved to have found Maci earlier. He only got to know her for a few weeks before he bit the dust."

A flood of memories hit me as Rowan continued to come down on my father for his very flawed plan. *What if we'd never met at all?* I didn't care for the idea of that. Most of my memories of human-Maci's life were a bit of a blur. I could call them up, but it was as if I watched them through a viewfinder from a distance away. I could see the memories, but I couldn't quite touch them, and I didn't care that much about them. I had a general sense of things, but Rowan said *bit the dust. That wasn't what his human-self did. He died in a coffin, slowly, while I died inside watching it.*

These memories didn't feel like someone else lived them. They were right there for me to access, as though I'd been there when it happened. All of that pain. The guys lived it, too. Abuse. Witnessing horror. Her human life hadn't been the only one to be wrapped up in a bed of nails she had to constantly roll around in.

I lifted my head to regard my father. "Well, it worked."

Rowan had been in the middle of saying something, and

I interrupted. My tolerance for the conversation was at about a zero, and I wasn't sure I could take any more.

"What worked?" My father blinked.

"You and my mother and all of the others, you went ahead and made us. That's what you wanted. We carry the memories that, for some reason, you all felt it was important that we have. I'm not exactly sure why you thought it would matter. To be honest with you, they seem to be the memories of a pretty normal woman. A vampire. She had loves, and she wanted to live her life the best way she knew how. Instead, Frederick wanted her, and he couldn't have her, so she was burned alive until she wasn't anything anymore." My hands shook as I spoke. "We're all just ordinary, aren't we? Sure, Rowan probably has some battle knowledge or maybe Ace does, but what does it matter? With all the fighting you've been doing, you probably have it, too." I held up my hand. I was on a rant, and I knew it. "So, congratulations! We're here. We're pretty normal, but I'm not going to live like this. I'm *absolutely* not going to. Rowan and I are going to do what we have to do, and then I'm going to go kill Frederick and the others. Thanks for all the effort you put into having me, but we're never going to have a relationship. As far as I'm concerned, it's just the six of us. The rest of the world doesn't matter to me anymore."

My father sighed. "Maci…"

I didn't want to hear it. "I would've died a human—and never been me—if you hadn't snuck me blood for years. Thanks for that," I called over my shoulder. Human-Maci had no idea what was happening to her, but I could remember those moments quite well. *It must be the vampire in me.* The only thing I knew for sure was I had to be away from my father acting like he hadn't played as much of a role in the situation as Frederick and the others. Manipulation was everywhere.

Caesar ran after me, catching up to be right by my side. Tanner was quickly on the other side. I'd been rude, and I supposed we were guests. The realization didn't bother me. If we had to leave, it might be better. We were predators, and I was pretty sure we could figure out how to survive without him.

"What you said was true," Tanner said quickly. "I don't have any particularly helpful skills that can add to anything."

Griffin caught up to Caesar's side. "Maybe we should just ask Frederick. I mean, I don't want to, because I hate the guy as much as any of you, but, fuck. He knows what the prophecy said, and he knows what he wanted from us. Your father, Maci, has no idea. He just wanted to thwart Frederick. He doesn't even know what he betrayed, which seems odd for a person being called the Betrayer."

Rowan suddenly joined us. They were faster than me, that much I was sure of. I needed to remember that in case anyone ever had to run for help, since it would be better if it wasn't me.

"Maci," Rowan grabbed my arm. "Come on. Let's do what we need to do to finish this whole process. Then we can all meet up and discuss what to do next. If we're attacking Frederick, we can't just knock on the front door and shoot him."

He had a point. We might be chosen or gifted or whatever, but we didn't even know how or what our supposed gifts did.

I squeezed Caesar's arm. "I'll be okay with Rowan."

"I'll be nearby anyway." He kissed my cheek. It was a

gentle move for him. "I'm never waking up again to find you've battled other vampires while I snored."

I smirked at him. "You weren't snoring, if that helps."

"It doesn't. It really doesn't, Maci." He rolled his eyes. "Take my point."

"There's nothing we can do about the sun, Caesar. You won't be able to stay up during daylight until you're able. That's just how it's going to go. No need to beat yourself up about it. Ace can. I can. We're it for right now. Frederick lost. I doubt he'll try a daytime attack again. No, the next time will be nighttime with his entire force behind him. It's either that or we attack him." I shook my head. "It doesn't matter which currently. I was pretty tough."

"Of course you were. You shouldn't have to be, though." He sighed. "We've never, not once, been able to keep you safe or keep you happy. It's always pain and running around. I can't imagine you'll want to stay if this keeps up."

Was that what he was worried about? I leaned in close to whisper in his ear. "Just try to get rid of me."

He smiled slowly. "I'd never do that."

I moved back but Griffin tugged on my sleeve. "I'm going to find out that prophecy tonight."

That was an abrupt shift I hadn't seen coming. "How are you going to do that?"

By way of an answer, Griffin lifted his eyebrows. "Trust me?"

A question for a question. That was never good. But I realized that I did trust Griffin as though I'd known and done so for many lives. I nodded. "Be careful. The prophecy isn't worth your life. I honestly don't give a shit what it says."

"I do." He kissed my other cheek then the one that Caesar had pressed his lips against. "And you know this about me. I can't leave this."

That was true. Tanner didn't kiss me, but his gaze traveled with me when I walked over to Rowan until I left his sight. He was less predictable than the others. I wasn't entirely sure what Tanner would do right then. He might sit down and do nothing or the entire battle could be over when I reemerged, with every possibility in between as well. Caesar would wait for me. He wouldn't move until I returned to him. If Ace was awake, he'd be rip roaring ready to go battle Frederick.

But he needed to speak with his mother. I would push him on that. I'd speak to mine too, eventually, if for no other reason than to tell them to leave us alone. They hadn't raised us, not even the ones who had been present. They barely kept the guys alive. We owed them nothing. The part of me that liked to cause pain—and that part definitely existed since I awoke—wanted to find them just to tell them to fuck off.

I'd see how much I felt like controlling myself.

It would depend. Maybe on the day. Or the minute.

I followed Rowan into one of the smaller bedrooms. He closed the door and, without a word, drew all the shades closed.

Rowan wasn't overly sentimental, so I didn't think he intentionally cocooned us in a silent world where only we existed. "You okay?" I asked as I walked toward him, stopping before I touched him.

He visibly swallowed. "I don't like feeding in front of others. I don't even like them knowing that I'm feeding particularly from you. What happens when I feed from you feels like it should be private. I know I have to get over it, and I've obviously gotten past my hang-ups in the past, but if I have a choice, I'd like to keep what happens between us private. Even if they know about it, they don't have to be privy to every detail. I would like some intimacy."

I was pretty sure I understood. "The things that happen to you when you feed from me? That's what you don't want to share?"

He nodded. "Maybe I brought some issues with me from being a human. Vampires don't care about privacy at all."

"There's no one voice for their vampires. I don't feel the same way about things that Caesar does. Or that Griffin does. He's trying to find a prophecy that I don't think is particularly useful, but it matters to him. If you prefer to feel sexual when we're alone, then so be it. I don't think you need to place judgment on your own feelings. I think they are just what they are, and that's all there is to it. Period, end of story, but that's just my opinion. As I said, there's no one right answer. Feel as you want to feel."

He quirked his mouth into an almost smile. "Did you really just give me permission to feel how I wanted to feel?"

"Well, you seemed to need it." I grabbed him and let him tug me against him. "Is that all that's bothering you?"

He shook his head. "No, but you really don't want to hear more."

"Yes, I do." I meant it. I offered him my neck. If he wanted to feed first and talk later, that was fine, too.

He ran his nose over my neck, right where my pulse would be. I closed my eyes, and he breathed me in, his soft exhale lifting the small hairs near my nape and making me shiver. "I don't want to lead. I know I was born for it, placed in my pre-determined role because of Frederick and also because of whoever this guy is that I'm carrying around. But I don't want it. I never did, not as a human or now. Ace would be better at the job." He sighed. "*You'd* be much better at it than any of us."

I opened my eyes to stare at him. "If I led, would you have my back? Every step of the way?"

"You think Caesar is attentive? You have no idea how fucking there I can be for you if I don't have to figure out how to lead us here there and everywhere. I'll be so there for you, no one will get near you if you don't want them around. They'll find themselves without their heads before they make it to you."

This was an entirely new side to Rowan. I grinned at him. "I think they can keep their heads. Well...maybe they can."

"Give me back your neck, Maci."

He might not want to lead, but he clearly didn't mind ordering me around. I obeyed him happily, and he didn't wait, he bit down on me. I shuddered against him, nearly coming in my pants. I was worked up, and his bite was the relief I needed. Rowan's mouth on my skin, his teeth digging into me. Fuck, it was so hot. It wasn't supposed to be. We were on a mission to travel through memories or whatever, but I couldn't help how he made me feel.

I ran my hands over his chest and held onto his shirt. He finally let go, licking my wound closed. "There's something else I don't like."

My eyes had closed as he sucked on me, and I hadn't even realized it. I opened them. "What's that?"

"I don't like you not being naked right this second."

I let him push me down on the bed roughly and grinned up at him. "So demanding tonight, Rowan, with all your preferences. Want to know one of mine?"

His smile was huge. "Absolutely."

"I'd like you to also be completely naked."

His smile fell. The moment became heavy, weighted with tension. It was serious. It meant something, what we were saying to each other, even if I wasn't entirely sure what any of it meant. I just knew that it would be *something*. Like I could feel the tingling in the room, speaking to the moment, almost like the very bell of fate rang in my ear.

Or maybe I was just a lunatic vampire who had no idea what was going on.

We both stripped quickly. Our gazes remained locked, and I didn't let myself look away. He held my gaze as intently as I did his. When I would have taken off my bra, he stopped me by catching my hands. "I want to do that."

I didn't respond because he undid the center clasp of my bra before I could. Rowan was completely exposed to me. If I looked down, his cock would stand proudly waiting for me, but I still couldn't drop my gaze from his.

"You wanted something from me when you were a human. I didn't understand it then, didn't think I could give you what you wanted. I was wrong. I will not let you down as a vampire."

I wasn't sure what he was talking about, and I didn't want to think about any of the human-Maci's disappointments right then. "Let's be here right now. We're predators. We live in the moment, right?"

He took my cheeks in his hands. "Not true and you know it."

I didn't know what I would have said in response, because his mouth touched my own and I exploded in heat, like I'd stepped into a fire.

Rowan was right. That wasn't true. Yes, I was a predator, but I was also a lover. I could be both.

And with Rowan, I really was both.

He wanted me to be in charge except for in his bed. "Maci." His voice rumbled low and deep, matching the way his mouth caressed mine. "Grab onto the headboard and don't let go. Before you bite me, I'm going to own you. You'll love every second of it."

I smiled at him. "Not that I'm complaining, but I thought that we were just getting our memories worked out. Have we both fallen off track?"

"Once I have you alone, I lose track of everything outside of what is between us. And tonight, I plan to take advantage of that weakness in myself as much as I possibly can."

It was such a different Rowan. It was as if, since he'd been given the freedom to express himself, and I'd listened to him, he became suddenly ravenously affectionate.

I couldn't say I minded. And it turned out that, like Rowan, I didn't want to think of anything outside of what was between us, either.

12

My senses were consumed by Rowan. He pushed my legs apart and met my pussy with his tongue in one eager swipe. I moaned, pleasure surging through me in a rush that stole my breath away. I clawed at my own arms, wanting pain to counteract the sheer bliss that rolled through me. Rowan grabbed my hand and placed it on his back. My monster moved inside of me. Yes, he knew what I wanted. I needed to administer pain, and he wanted to take it.

I loved Rowan so fucking much. Digging my fingers into his back, I wasn't gentle. He raised his mouth and lifted his head to look at me, his eyes gone a bloody red. Our monsters regarded each other easily. His was stronger, but he loved me. He wanted to give me what I wanted...to a point.

"Take me. *Now*." I lifted an eyebrow. Would he comply?

Rowan flipped me over. He was going to do as I instructed, but he'd do it his way. I gripped the headboard. He touched me one more time before he pressed inside of me. "You are so wet for me."

"I think... " I began, then caught my breath as my body adjusted to him. " ...under the circumstances, that's a very good thing, don't you?"

He pushed in and out of me, one stroke after another, over and over. Each delicious slide urged my senses higher until I felt drunk on lust. Rowan didn't answer me, and that was fine. The time for talking was done. We moved as a single unit. He pushed; I pressed. I'd no sooner think I understood what was happening, that I could anticipate what was next, than he'd adjust his hips and it would all start over. I panted, small grunts of noise coming helplessly out of my throat, when he finally jerked hard against my spot, making me shudder and finally come around him. I leaned forward, unable to stop myself and would have hit the headboard if his hand hadn't been right there to stop me from colliding.

I had a second to smile, wondering how quickly I could get better from a head injury as a vampire, when he bit down on my neck. *Yes.* I loved that, but it wasn't what we needed. Somewhere in my pleasure-hazed brain I remembered that. I had to feed from him. I wrenched my neck back. Confusion warred over his gaze for just a second before I bit his neck and fed. *Yes, I fucking love this.* My muscles clenched and pleasure flooded me before I drifted back into the memories of a woman I'd been born to know. I wouldn't have chosen our connection, and I doubted she had known anything about it, but we were linked, regardless.

She turned around, and I caught a glimpse of her in the mirror. She was younger than when I saw her before. Quickly, she walked to the door, and like the observer-slash-parasite I was in these moments, I went along while she swung it open. Rowan—the version of him there—leaned against the outdoor frame, staring at me.

His face spread in a big grin of greeting. "Hi."

She sighed, and her joy moved through me. "You came."

"Well, of course I did." He walked past me into the house. "The others would never have forgiven me if I didn't. Before we met you, I swear we all used to be reasonable, but now that we've met, we're all lunatics to be around you all of the time."

I smiled back at him. It wasn't the first time I'd heard them describe how they felt about me. *Her*. I blinked. It was harder than it should have been to keep my head separated in Rowan's memory. Most of the other times had all been so angst-filled, but she was so happy in that moment. Real happiness, not even tempered by any of the vampire sourness that rode me most of the time. She was truly happy in that second—like, human levels of happy.

They took it for granted, I realized. They expected to have the ability to feel things acutely and purely without having to navigate around the monster inside of them. Or at least they could feel that way sometimes. It wasn't always, because they could experience the full range of emotions, but it stunned me that they could feel unbridled joy. It was the only description I could even begin to explain how she felt right then.

She tugged on her Rowan's shirt. "I feel it, too. The connection. The way vampires can feel if they're lucky? I feel it with you. With all of you." I wanted him to kiss me right then more than I'd ever desired anything in my whole life.

He took my cheeks in his hands, a gentle caress of warmth and strength. "If you let me, I'll make you feel like this forever. Nothing will ever happen to you."

She didn't know it, but I was sure, because I knew the future—he wouldn't be able to keep that promise.

But oh how happy she'd been right then.

I was flung back into my body, and Rowan's arms came around me. He held me close, rocking me gently. I liked him better than I liked his counterpart. He didn't make promises that were impossible to keep. I actually appreciated that he saw how hard life could be and walked that road anyway instead of pretending to be upbeat all the time. That wasn't real. Whatever kind of vampire I was, it wasn't the optimistic, shiny magical-thinking kind.

I was the *I need to blow those fuckers up* variety of vampire.

Rowan helped me to lift my head. I blinked, my vision finally clearing enough to really look at him. "I'm so glad that's over."

"What did you see?"

"A moment they shared in the hall. He professed his love for her and promised he'd keep her safe forever."

Rowan nodded. "Interesting. I got the entire picture of his life. While he was a nice guy, he was completely blindsided by what life threw at him. I won't be that way, but I've come to believe it won't be me keeping us all safe. I think that's going to be you. You're just too powerful for it to be otherwise. Maci, you should barely be conscious in a need for blood, and I can see that your brain is plotting. You stayed up all day and barely slept, yet you look perfectly fine. It isn't normal. I think...I think if there is part of her in you, then she came back because she's got serious unfinished business, and she's not willing to wait to finish things up."

I kissed the end of his nose. "That's me, not her. She's there, but I'm the one in charge here."

I wanted to be perfectly clear about that. This was my show, not the ghosts of the past. What happened with her? It just made me madder.

DAYTIME MUST HAVE COME, because I woke up when the sun set. I yawned and lifted my head. Rowan still slept beside me. The sunrise took us both down, and I'd done nothing to stop it. Ace stared down at me from the end of the bed.

He rocked back on his feet. "I guess I slept through the whole day."

"You did." I nodded. "And that's fine."

He smirked at me, a familiar Ace expression that said he knew I wasn't saying everything I should. My monster roared to life, awakening to greet his. Usually, that was saved for Tanner, but she liked the way Ace challenged us. My nipples hardened. I'd love to have the time to just pounce on him, but it wasn't going to happen today. There were things to do.

Even if he has really nice cheekbones and abs under his shirt that would be fun to stroke.

I got up on my knees. "I'm going to shower and feed Tanner and then we should talk about stuff that happened yesterday. Maybe we can make some time to see your mother before we figure out how to end this mess. Sound good?"

Rowan groaned. "You don't really ease into the day, do you? It's like up and at it."

I shook my head. "Why bother with baby steps?"

"That could be your whole motto as a vampire: *nothing in small doses.*" He lifted himself up on his elbows. "Ace, how did you get in here? I thought I locked the door."

Ace held up his hand, showing them both the door handle he held in his long, elegant fingers. "I removed the barrier. I refuse to be locked away from her. Caesar either. You had one night, so I've been informed. It's a new one. See you later, Maci." He looked over his shoulder as he exited. "I'm not the least bit interested in meeting my mother."

I stood up, stretching. "You're eventually going to have to meet her, you know that, right? If you don't want to now, that's fine, but you're going to have to deal with her at some point. She lives right over there." I pointed in what I was pretty sure was the general direction of her house. "I dealt with my father, so you can do the same."

"I'd rather move. Or burn down the entire house."

That was so dramatic, it might be funny...if only I wasn't absolutely certain he was serious. Griffin rushed through the door before I could say more. His eyes were huge, and he darted from one foot to the next, the most animated I had seen him with my vampire eyes. "Did you get it?"

He held up the book. "I did." As he spoke, Tanner joined us. They all clearly were tired of waiting around. He snuggled up next to me, and I bit down on his neck. His sigh moved through me while I drank and listened to Griffin speak. "I spent my daylight hours in a random trailer in the woods, even though I've never done that before. It was so exciting. I stole from the elders, and then I was practically exposed to the sun. It was...*exhilarating*. Anyway, here." He held up the book. "I've read it."

I grinned as I released Tanner's neck. *Of course he finished reading it already*. In every lifetime, Griffin succeeded in whatever he attempted.

He asked, "Is everyone ready to hear about the prophecy?"

"If we have to." Caesar leaned against the doorway. "I'd

rather talk about Maci's tits, but yeah, sure, we can talk about prophecy, if that's what floats your boat."

Tanner groaned. "You're going to want to talk about it, Caesar. I have a feeling it'll be what sets Maci in motion, burning all those fuckers to the ground." His monster flew to the surface of his eyes as he spoke. Tanner liked that idea, and his monster loved it.

So the fuck do I.

I licked his wound closed. "I want to hear about the prophecy."

"Well, it's not our prophecy. You heard that, about us returning in new bodies or some shit to be great leaders. Honestly, feels like bullshit to me. I haven't seen that one, and why would that be, I wonder? I can't deny we're all carrying these memories, and it's not like that's typical. No other vampires are resurrected from the past, so I guess that prophecy came true or whatever."

Rowan cleared his throat. "First of all, we don't know what other vampires are and are not carrying. We activated each other's memories with blood. We're also soul mates. Well, all of us with her, not necessarily with each other. Vampires aren't doing that anymore, so who knows what the norm is? I certainly don't. Secondly, get out of my bedroom, let Maci take a shower, and then we'll do this. She might also like to feed. And that is my last order, because she's in charge from now on."

They all turned to stare at me. "Unless someone wants to object," Rowan added.

"You're in charge, fine." Caesar met my gaze. "But I'm still going to keep you safe whether you like it or not, even if you tell me not to."

I stretched my arms over my head. "I get to keep you

safe, too, Caesar. All of you. Yes, let me shower, then we'll talk prophecy. I'm not the least bit hungry. I can't make sense of why I am sometimes and why I'm not other times."

"It's because you're miraculous." Tanner winked at me. "Trust me on that."

In that moment, his monster was nowhere to be found. Just Tanner—practically the human Tanner I'd once known —and in that second, I was Maci from then, too. We stared at each other, familiarity so strong, I could practically curl into it. It wasn't so obvious with the others. Did they notice it? That my human-self had just temporarily asserted herself into my person? Why had that happened?

And what does that mean that it did?

I headed for the bathroom, the questions I had no answers for riding me the whole way.

THE SHOWER RINSED AWAY my sweat but not my worries. The human side receded some, which let me think clearly again. She wasn't riding my brain, and that was a good thing. Too much pain and sentimentality weren't called for in these moments. I dressed in a pair of yoga pants and a t-shirt, preferring comfort and the ability to move over anything sexy or alluring. Other women might want to look lovely.

That had never been me.

The guys were in the living area. Caesar leaned against the doorway closest to me. I wrapped my hand around his bicep for a second as I passed by him. He was strong, his skin warm and smooth, and I loved that. Eventually, I flopped down on the couch. I could feel all of them watching me, their gazes heavy enough to carry actual weight. In any other circumstance, I'd be thrilled to just spread my legs and let each one of them come at me.

In fact, I hadn't really gotten to have sex with Griffin since my rising. We would have to do something about that. He was so sexy. I shook my head. I had to focus. I might be a sex addict, but if I wanted to burn down Frederick's world, I needed to pay attention to Griffin's brain, not his biceps.

For a little bit, anyway.

He held up the book. "This book claims to be able to break the history of vampires into sections. Beginnings and endings, and they call them prophecies. I guess that is what they are . I haven't had a lot of spare time in my life to worry about things like mumbo jumbo, but if we believe it, the book says there will be a great war. The ones who have embraced the vampires who hold onto the past will win it."

I waited for more. When Griffin didn't say anything else, I leaned forward. "What else does it say?"

"It goes on to talk about the reincarnation. Holding the memories of those who lived in the past. It's not necessarily that we *are* them so much as we were born carrying their understandings like a road map. Those people are dead, long dead. The feeling we have where we're not them? Yes, that's absolutely accurate. We're not them, and we never were them. We've seen their stories now, but they're not our memories, and we may never be able to access them again." He shook his head. "But we're supposed to be able to win the war for them, even though it isn't our war. Regardless of the winner, the war sets a new era of vampirism in motion. That's what it says. Frederick wants to be the leader of that era. He's even made notes in the book." Griffin held it up again, gesturing to the page to prove his point. "He thinks he's started that with the changes he made, like there is no way that it can be undone or something. He thinks he thwarted the whole thing."

I rose. "Okay, so what I'm hearing is there is no great revelation in the prophecy. We knew this stuff already, or at least most of it. There is no huge information dump. Here's what I want to know, Ace, are your parents soul mates? Go over there and find out if they share memories with dead people. Maybe it's common and just no one talks about it, like sex or something like that."

"Do we not talk about sex?" Griffin scrunched up his face.

"Humans don't." Tanner shrugged. "I'm happy to talk about it if the subject ever comes up."

Ace groaned. "That was a dirty trick right there, Maci. Now I have no choice but to go talk to the woman."

I shook my head. "I wish I could say that I planned it, but I didn't. It's just my good luck that it worked out."

"Damn it." He walked toward the door. "No one make battle plans until I get back."

"So what do you want to do?" Caesar kissed my cheek. "What is our next move?"

"Tanner," I took his hand. "Go, see my Dad. I want to know how many people we have who would be willing to fight. I want numbers, then we'll plot." I walked to the window to look outside. I needed to access the memories of one very ordinary vampire woman so I could win some kind of war. If Ace's parents weren't also getting those memories, then the difference had to be in that ability. Why did it matter? Or had it never mattered, and only started to because Frederick had made a thing out of it?

He nodded. "Sure. I'm not usually the one sent to talk. I love it. I'll do it." My sometimes-silent soul mate tore from the room.

I pointed at the book. "Griff, are there other prophecies? I mean things that people have thrown out because they were meaningless, or they didn't come true?"

He blinked. "Yes, actually. We had to study all of those books before we turned. There were some nonsensical things that are nothing." He took a beat. "Oh, I see what you're saying."

Caesar yawned. "I don't. Somebody fill me in."

"Did this book have any real meaning before someone attributed meaning to it? Like he read it and decided it was real."

He followed exactly what I was thinking. "If other soul mates carry memories that no one talks about, and anyone who would know about coming back with memories has since died—Frederick doesn't have one, so he doesn't know that..."

"We're literally at war over something that doesn't matter."

Rowan paced to the window to stare bleakly outside. "Maybe that's true of most wars. Maybe most things are nonsense if you take the time to really look at them."

"We still have to win the war, even if it is meaningless." I realized as I spoke the words that I absolutely meant them. "He has to be stopped. We'll complete the prophecy by ushering in a new non-Frederick- led generation of vampires who can hopefully do better."

Griffin set down the book on the table. "Look, our girl is an optimist."

I couldn't stop eyeing him, and it wasn't going to get any better. I'd sent Ace out on a mission, which meant I had enough time to thank Griffin for getting the book, personally.

"Hey, Griff," I said as I shot a smile at him. "Want to talk about sex? With me? Right now?"

He opened and closed his mouth. "Sure. Absolutely. Right here? In the room with all of them?"

"No, although I would be open minded about discussing that on another night. For tonight, how about you and I go talk about sex in another bedroom?"

His monster rose to the surface to regard me. It was such an unusual moment for Griffin, because he kept his beast so tightly leashed most of the time, I hardly ever saw him. But there he was, smiling back at me. Griffin sometimes forgot how physical of a creature he was. The cerebral was great, but Griff needed to remember to let his monster come out and play.

"Actually," I took his hand and brought it to my mouth, "you can have me...*if* you can catch me."

I didn't give him the chance to answer. I stalked Tanner, but Griffin would have to find me. Caesar and Rowan would hate me running off, because they didn't want me out of sight for safety, but I didn't care right then. My need for Griffin got to win over their need to suppress my wildness.

I took off running, pleased as the muscles bunched and stretched in my legs. I got a chance to get to know the layout of the area when we battled Fredrick's goons, so I ran everywhere I could think of, not stopping for even a second. Griffin was faster than me, but I could out dodge him. We ran for at least a half an hour before I spun around a corner and he tackled me to the ground. Before I would have impacted, he rolled beneath me to take the brunt of the force and then rolled us both over so he was on top. His fangs were elongated, and his eyes were red. Oh yes, I'd awoken the monster inside of Griffin.

And it was *so* hot.

"You're not scared of me when I'm like this, and it makes me hot. It makes me want you even more, and I always wanted you. When I was human and now, there is nothing I want more than you all of the time." He bit down on my neck. I cried out for him, clutching to keep him close. I had no warning before he struck, and that was fine by me. Let him take what he wanted from me, because I would give him everything.

We stripped each other quickly, having no use for barriers between us. We rolled around, desperate for each other's pleasure and greedily seeking more and more. I was on top and then he was. He reached down, finding my clit deftly and stroking it. I rubbed against his hand, seeking more, and he moaned.

"Griffin, you can't break me. Fuck me as hard as you want for as long as you want right here on the ground."

He kissed my cheeks. "Yes. Right now."

He pushed himself inside of me roughly. We ended up against a tree, the bark digging into my back. It cut me, probably leaving wounds on my back. I fucking loved it.

Griffin lost control as if the scent of my blood on the night air drove him wild, and I held on for the ride. Waves of pleasure arched through me over and over again. I cried out, moaning, thrashing against him until I finally found my release. I held onto his neck, trembling in aftershocks, and he ground into me. Yes, we'd needed this. Tears rushed from my eyes, and I let them fall. *What an amazing release.*

We were vampires.

Sometimes we just needed to fuck each other, particularly when there was danger coming and we were in love.

I blinked at the thought. *We are, aren't we?*

Lifting my head, I stared at him as he panted above me. "Do you love me?"

Griffin's vampire retreated, going back where he held him at bay most of the time. "I do. I've never been warm, not in any manifestation, but I love you, Maci, with everything in me that can love."

I kissed his cheek. "Griff, you can't possibly think you're cold, not after you just broke that tree fucking me against it."

His smile was huge. "I did, didn't I?"

Yes, he had.

13

Ace wasn't okay. He'd been gone too long, and his distress ached in my bones. As a human, I knew if they were not all right. It hadn't traveled exactly over with me, but some of it was coming back. I sent him to meet his mother, so it was my fault if things went terribly wrong.

With Caesar by my side, I spotted the situation from a distance. His father stood with Ace's mother. He had been such a complete mystery to me, and although I had some answers about why that was—he fell in love with Ace's mother, and they were soul mates. He'd lied and tricked Frederick for her—I still wasn't clear on all of his motives. Neither was Ace, and the stress pulsating off my love wasn't good.

Ace tended to let his fury out in fiery explosions.

"Hi," I said as I slid my arm around Ace's waist. Caesar nodded to me from his other side. If the others knew he was in bad shape, they would've shown up, too. It was an hour until daytime, so he should've returned to us a long time ago, if he'd just been visiting his mother to ask about past life visions.

However, his father's presence changed things drastically. There was a whole hill of pain from his human days there, and maybe some since he was a vampire, too.

They all turned to look at me, and his mother tried to force her lips into the semblance of a smile. Ace shot daggers at his father, but he said, "You're here just in time to hear about why he did the things he did. He's been away, but now that he thinks we're about to go to war, he's come out of hiding. Great timing, right?"

Ace's father glared back at him. "Don't presume to know what I have and haven't been doing. I lived with those monsters for years. I did it to stay with you and to protect your mother." The couple looked at each other, gentleness hitting his gaze for the first time. "And I've stayed away, because if they're looking for me, and they are, I didn't want them to find your mother. At this point, you can handle yourself, maybe even better than I can, since you're awake in daylight while you should still be passing out early every night."

"I can do a lot more than just stay up." For a second, a dangerous glint lit his gaze, but then he shook his head. "Never mind. What I can and can't do is none of your business, but you're going to have to excuse it if I hold onto some judgment of you. I've recently learned from Griffin how you impregnated women and then had them killed because Frederick ordered it, so you don't have any moral high ground to stand on with me."

Ace's father looked down, unhappiness clear on his face. "I am deeply ashamed of those years. They were confusing. I had worries about Frederick, but he was powerful, and all the elders were dead. We followed him, everyone followed. He seemed right, and we were getting more and more powerful. Towns full of people did what we wanted, but there was part of me that remained uneasy. I did those terrible things. I did. Then I met your mother, and it was like I woke up. She was mine, my soul mate, my everything. I wouldn't let anyone hurt her or take our baby, no matter what Frederick thought. As soon as you were born, when he ordered the women killed, I hid your mother away. I gave him the body of a random woman who had died from using drugs. He never noticed, since they were all the same to him. I brought your mother here, and we changed her. Warren agreed to keep her safe so long as I played ball and kept you safe once you were born, so that's what I did. Go ahead and judge once you've been a vampire for more than two seconds." He pointed at Ace. "*You* were the most perfect vampire I'd ever met. You did everything they tasked you to do and then some. I wasn't about to spill my guts to a person who was basically responsible for destroying anyone that pissed Rowan off for months. Don't act holier than thou, Ace. You won't like how you come off in that argument."

"Okay." I put my hand on Ace's arm. "I appreciate that you never fed from me. I'll say thank you for that, but Ace had a fucked-up childhood. He has lots of reasons to feel the way he does, and it isn't fair for you to belittle or disregard his experiences. He is entitled to his anger about your behavior as well. He's one of the best people I know. Whatever you think you know about him, you don't, but right now, I don't care about any of it. Whether you're all bad people, bad vampires, mean, rude or whatever is not my concern. What I want to know is whether or not you two see past lives. Do you?"

They stared at each other, and his mother visibly swallowed. "No. Is that something you can do? Is that something that *actually* happened to all of you?"

"Thank you." I wasn't in the mood to answer her questions.

Ace and Caesar followed me as I walked away. *When this is over, I'm done with almost everyone else.* We could live somewhere by ourselves doing our own things and everyone else could live with their decisions and what they did and didn't do. I had my own regrets, lifetimes of them. I was tired of carrying around the burden of everyone else's mistakes.

"Maci," Rowan said as he ran out the door. "That feeling I got last time? I have it again. They're coming."

With almost no time left before the sunrise, they were coming. They'd have a full complement of vampires with them, and then the sun would come out. It would thin us out, because more of them could stay awake than we could. We'd be overrun—it was actually really good strategy.

My mind pinged. They had to be stopped before they arrived. The constant fighting in the fields hadn't worked, and fighting here was fruitless. They just had so many more people than we did. It would be a bloodbath, and we'd be the ones drowning instead of reveling in it.

I turned back to Caesar. "Get everyone out of here. Everyone who lives here, I want them lined up away from here in that field. You know, over where you fought them when you were hiding me when I was a human."

He scowled at me. "I'm not going to leave you, Maci."

"No, you're not. Absolutely, you're not. But I need you to get my father and everyone else out. After you've done that, come back to me. We have things to do here."

He nodded. "Okay. That I can do."

Ace was next.

I said to him, "He burned that woman to death. The one whose memory I carry? He burned her like she was nothing." I chewed on my lip, determination stiffening my spine. "He isn't going to get the chance to do that to anyone here. I don't know what we're going to do yet, but as long as we have this large group hanging around, I am going to be responsible for them. Get them away, Ace. His battle can't be with them."

His battle was with me.

~

Ace

THE CONVERSATION with my father had thrown me. I'd been prepared for my mother but not my father. *Fuck him.* He was bad, even by vampire standards, and I'd be happy to be rid of him. How dare he judge me? I'd gone out of my way to control my bad nature. I even lied when it was supposed to be impossible. My father was the nightmare.

End of story.

But Maci gave me something to do, so I was going to do it. Whatever she wanted or needed, she would have it. I stopped in front of Warren's place.

I hated the man. With a vengeance.

When we'd first arrived, it had been hell to deal with him.

I hardly let myself think about that night anymore, but right then, my memories flooded me, whether I wanted them to or not.

We'd followed my father's directions, leaving our car miles away and walking the rest of the way. Warren must have known we were coming, because he stood outside with a female vampire. They both silently regarded us, and I must have looked like I'd been dragged from the pits of hell, because even though they checked out all of us, they couldn't take their eyes off me. I challenge them to know how great they looked if Maci had died on their watch.

She was my...I didn't even know how to phrase it.

"You've had a bad night," Warren said in a low voice. "I can understand. You didn't know she was being dosed with my blood. You thought she was gone permanently, which would be a blow, since you love her." He put his arm around the female next to him. I'd never seen a female vampire before, but she just looked normal, just like us, really. Not quite human, something other, and more like one of us than any human woman did.

Would Maci look like that?

"If we didn't know that she was going to return, we would've been wrecked, too."

Fury rose inside me like electricity I couldn't turn off. "How *dare* you act parental? Whatever you are, you aren't a father. Not a real one." Were all vampire parents that fucked up? "She barely survived her childhood. Whatever game this is you've been playing, you're disgusting."

Rowan cleared his throat then said, "My friend is exhausted. He's been up for over twenty-four hours. At this moment, he has no tact, and I'm grateful for it. You are all those things he said. Why are we here? I don't want anything to do with you. Just give me her location so I can wait there until she returns."

"If I knew it, I'd give it to you. I've never been privy to Frederick's dumping grounds. Funny, he calls himself that now. For years it was Edwin, his middle name. I guess he's comfortable going back to the original name now. After he did some things, he changed it to Edwin." He shook his head. "You love her. Come inside. We'll get you set up in a house where you can be comfortable. When she rises, one way or another, you'll find her or she'll find you. Maci is not lost to time. She will return to you."

"Love?" It was Caesar who spoke. "Vampires don't love."

Warren sighed. "Yes, we do. We don't just love, we love eternally. Soul mates. Some of us have more than one, as is the case with all of you. You love her completely. Instantly. Both as humans and now, so strongly I can see it. How can you not? You must feel it. The all-consuming-ness of her. You don't even need to feed from humans anymore. You can feed just from each other."

Griffin visibly swallowed. "This wasn't what we were taught."

"Well...they lied to you. Constantly. My poor daughter. Did she not know she was loved?"

That was the hit that broke me that day. I'd been up too long, and Warren was right—much as I hated him. Maci never knew how much I loved her. My knees gave way, and I would have fallen if Caesar and Rowan hadn't caught me.

Her father stared at me. "How are you even awake during the daytime? You shouldn't be able to do it for years to come."

That was always the million-dollar question, not that we ever had answers. I just fucking could.

Maci

"I WANT to be here when he arrives. I want the rest of you to be hidden away, just me." I sighed.

Rowan shook his head. "You don't actually think we're going to let you do that, do you?"

"I'm not saying actually leave, so you don't have to go far enough away to let me out of your sight. Just don't be visible. Let me talk to him alone. If he has a crowd around him, even better. Anyway, after that, while he thinks he's going to hurt all of us, the rest of the group will take over his home base."

It took a second, but Rowan's smile was huge. "Oust them from their home? Take it over. That's right. Let's see what happens when they're the ones not comfortable anymore."

Caesar shook his head. "They'll just stay here."

"Not easily. Burn what you can; destroy the rest. They can't stay easily if we remove their ability to shield from the day." I looked at Rowan. "Can you do that for me?"

He kissed me quickly. "I can. Whatever you want."

No way was I being separated from Caesar. I'd be lucky if he stayed out of sight like I asked him. I squeezed his hand as Rowan left. Where were Griffin and Tanner?

As though I'd conjured him, Tanner appeared. "What can I do?"

A good question, since it would take more than Rowan to trash the place. "Help Rowan destroy everything. Leave nothing where they can sleep well here. They'll have to hide in closets, crawl in corners like rats. After you're done, you and Ace go take back their homes for us. That'll mean you can't be here, so I'm counting on you, okay?"

If I hoped to get them to go, I needed them to believe it was worth it. And it was. If we had any chance of pulling off the plan, everything had to go right. So far, nothing we'd done particularly went the way we intended.

"It'll happen. I'll stay awake through the day until it's done. I can do it."

Rowan grabbed my arm. "We'll all make it. You can count on us, Maci. You can."

We could talk later about how it didn't make them less than anyone else because they were unable to stay awake, but I didn't have the time for it in the moment.

Griffin ran out of our house and into my vision as Rowan left with Tanner to do what I'd asked. "I found something. I swear whatever we just did by the tree woke up my brain, but I knew what book to look through." He held it up. "I think we should talk about this."

I wanted to hear what he found, but I wasn't sure we had time for reading hour. "Griff, we're about to go to battle. Is what you found relevant? I really want to know, but maybe later, after, unless it will help or hurt now?"

I hated saying no to him. Griffin was different from my other loves. He wasn't a fighter, although he could fight. He shook his head, grabbing my arm. "If fighting is coming, I want to get you out of here. I know the others." He shot Caesar a look. "And they think you can lead us. I know you can, and I'm not a coward, but we lost you. For nine fucking months, you were dead. We knew you'd be coming back, but, no, I don't want you to fight." He took a deep breath. "Okay. I've spoken my piece. None of you will care or agree with me on this subject, so I'll get on board. No, this book won't matter just now. But afterward, we really, really need to talk about it. How can I help?"

My heart turned over. I really fucking loved Griffin. Part of me wished I could be the girl who would run away. Even among vampires, we were different. Ace's mother hid away for years. How could she stand that? It would kill me. My own mother, who I still hadn't laid eyes on, abandoned me to some kind of plan by my father. What sort of person was she? It didn't matter. I was a fighter. I'd been born—reborn —that way.

I cupped his cheek. "Do you remember the test you gave me? The one about the standard miners?"

"Yes, and you asked me after I was reborn how I would handle it now. I told you. I'd kill the miner who was sick. It's the only sensible way to solve the problem. You had said the leader should kill themselves to save the rest."

That was exactly right. "Now? Since I've been reborn? My opinion has changed. If the leader got them stuck in there, then she or he deserves to kill themselves for the error because they were in charge. If I'm in charge, I'm going to see to it that we don't get stuck. If you want to help me, help Tanner and Ace get where we're headed set up. I'm counting on you. Yes, absolutely, afterward you will tell me about that book. I can't wait to hear about it."

He leaned over and kissed me. "I'd burn the world to the ground for you. I'm not some kind of vampire pacifist. I just want us. I don't care about everyone else. I know that it's not possible, but I would take you and keep you from them, if I could. That would be my preference."

"The goal is to just to make our family survive. I might get lost in doing this. Don't let me, okay?"

He kissed me again. "I won't, Maci. Make no mistake, I'll be right there next to you. Just do me a favor? Don't forget the house that we loved. When you were human, you loved that house. It was ours. We deserve the right to live when this is over. Not to take over for Frederick." He pointed at the book. "And that actually relates to this."

I couldn't wait to hear more.

14

The guys did as I asked. It was still dark when I stood with Caesar on top of a roof, staring down at the scene below. The other vampires were coming, so I hoped my guys were okay with the upcoming sun. A quick glance showed me Caesar was still upright, but for how long?

I didn't dare bring it up, not when I was doing such a good job of pretending to look bored.

I was absolutely not filled with ennui right then. Just the opposite, in fact. I'd never been so completely focused in my life.

Or my death.

Or since whatever it was at this point.

"Do you need to feed?" Caesar asked, nudging my shoulder with his own.

I nodded. "I'd love to feed, but now is definitely not the time. That's just for you and me, when it happens. I don't want to add it onto our night of the vampire damned or whatever we want to call it. Does that sound like a good movie title for this?"

He smirked. "I'd love to watch a movie sometime. I didn't mean me, actually. As much as it would pain me, I thought maybe you should feed from a human. Just enough to get you fed if not full, so to speak."

I'd fed from a human since my guys found me again. The buzzing noise in my head that signified their approach was too loud, too present. I touched a hand to my temple and said, "I think it's too late."

I spotted the vampires, and my spine stiffened. Frederick was in the back, following the other elders who fed from me constantly when I'd been their servant. They all made my human-self miserable, but they'd fathered all of my loves. Well, not Ace. His father was his own version of problematic, which was neither here nor there at the moment.

Fredrick snarled as he spotted me. The whole group moved like they were going to pound on the house, a sea of power and strength. I lifted my hand in the universal gesture for stop, and surprisingly, they all obeyed. *How interesting.* These vampires liked to take orders, but why shouldn't they? They'd only taken order after order since rising.

None of them understood how we were supposed to live, or how farcical they looked compared to what they could be. "Hi. My name is Maci," I began. I smiled like I was sweet. I was absolutely not sweet, but they didn't know that. Maybe I'd risen as Maci the friendly vampire? I couldn't help it. My nerves had my thoughts spinning in ridiculous directions. I cleared my throat and tried again.

"Some of you probably remember me from when I was human and you fed from me. I should have died then, but I didn't." I nodded toward Frederick. "I died when he killed me, instead. I don't actually remember it, but he clonked me over the head. Maybe I died then? Maybe it was later. Doesn't matter." I spun in a circle. "As you can see, I rose."

"What are you all doing?" Frederick snarled to his group. "Get her."

"They can try, but in a little bit." I shrugged. "The thing is I think you should hear some things before you do it. Just a few things, then by all means, come and get me."

Caesar made a noise. He didn't like me basically taunting them. That was okay. I didn't care for it much, either, but I had a plan, and so far it had played out just the way I wanted.

"He didn't want me reborn, because he didn't want me to know what I know. He didn't want me to have the capacity or knowledge to tell you how he burned a female vampire to death after she wouldn't have sex with him. How he altered the lives of all vampires everywhere because she said no to him." I shook my head. "He doesn't have a great sense of how vampires should live, not the least idea about it. But what Frederick knows is how he burned her to death. Afterward, he took all the women away from you. The Betrayer, as you call him? He fathered the human that was me and he lives with my mother, who he loves. Ace's father Vincent lives with the woman he loves. I live with the men I love."

There, I said my piece. Almost. "Oh, and Frederick, I know how much you like to burn people and things, so I thought I'd make you feel right at home. We're taking your home right now, while you stand here messing with me."

Caesar lit the large match he carried and dropped it straight onto the ground on top of the gasoline he'd put there minutes before. It wouldn't burn the place down, but it made them all dart back in terror. We all hated fire, a natural vampire instinct since it could destroy us.

For a second, I was frozen, staring into the blue heart of the flame, utterly transfixed. She burned and screamed in terror, the greedy flames gobbling her up one crackle at a time. The sound of her voice still reverberated in my ears as she screamed and screamed. I shook my head.

"Let's get out of here." I nodded at Caesar. Hopefully I'd wasted enough time for my guys to have accomplished the rest of the plan. The sun was going to be out, golden light scouring the earth soon.

He squeezed my hand, and we jumped down the other side of the house. "Remind me never to piss you off, Maci."

I grinned at him as we ran. "I'm scary, that's for sure."

He rolled his eyes. "Agreed, but I knew that before today. I'm just glad they all know it now, too."

So was I.

THEY TOOK the town with no issue whatsoever. The remaining vampires ran when they arrived, and most of the servants vanished, too. Only a few still lingered, and they weren't people I recognized. I didn't know if I should feel good or bad because the ones who were my friends were long gone. Were they dead, run off earlier, or had they preferred to stay with Frederick? I shook my head. I'd love to tell them straight out how the only ones who might ever make them vampires were with us.

But it didn't matter.

My father ran to me, grabbing my arms. "This was such a good idea. We should have done this years ago. They can't stay together today in comfort. Brilliant. This is why we needed you."

I shook my head. "This was one of my ideas. We need others, but not today. They're going to be pissed at rising, really mad, I can promise you that. We need to have the daywalkers patrol all day and the nightwalkers to take over at rising."

"On it." He nodded. "It'll be done."

I had to find my guys. I turned toward Caesar. "Hanging in?"

"You can count on me. I told you, stop worrying about me. It's my job to worry about you."

A sweet thought, but it didn't mean he wasn't suffering. I rounded the corner and headed straight for what had been Frederick's office. Since all of his books remained, I at least knew where Griffin would be.

I heard them before I saw them. All of them were in there.

"Hey," they cheered as I walked through the door. "It worked. It all worked."

Ace opened his arms, and I stepped into them. He kissed the top of my head. "Well done."

"It worked for now. It's not going to go away this easily. We've taken their stronghold, but we have to keep it, and then we have to kill them." I closed my eyes. "And all of you need to go to bed."

"You do, too." Rowan shook his head and took me from Ace. "Just because you can doesn't mean that you absolutely should stay awake. You had a long day. Go to bed. Wake in rising. There'll be plenty of battle waiting for you then."

I sighed. "You are actually the one with the battle memories. They wanted you for that, remember. You don't have to lead but what about the plan?"

He made a face. "That's part of what is so strange. I'm not that much of a battle genius. Never have been. I'm defunct that way."

I groaned. It was really awful when they doubted themselves, when they were critical of who they were. It was like pain when they criticized themselves.

I shook my head. "Who knows what you'd be able to do if you were allowed to be new vampires and not immediately sent into the game like you'd been drinking blood for years." I held up my hand. "We can discuss this another time. We need to go to bed. Feed. The whole nine yards. The good news is they need to do that too."

With various nods, they all started spreading out around Frederick's home. We were familiar with it. It was remarkably like his last home, which I cleaned many times. He was clearly the kind of person who liked things the way that he liked them. The guys spread out in Frederick's bedroom. He had fresh sheets on the bed and the couches covered in sheets too. The servants must have been preparing for bed before they'd taken off running, and the guys had probably spread the sheets themselves. I walked to the window and drew the curtains so we were in the dark.

Maybe I should stay up and be part of the daywalking guards? I just wouldn't tell my guys, so they wouldn't worry.

"Maci." Ace put out his hand. "You always feed us to sleep. We're going to do that for you today. You're not going out there, despite what you're thinking.

Damn it. Ace really was as devious as me. Two vampires who could lie when so few could, and we were together. The whole world was going to be constantly suspicious of us, and they probably should be.

I scowled at him. "I think maybe I..."

He shook his head. "I think if you don't sleep, you can't battle tomorrow."

Griffin rubbed at his eyes. "And we have to talk about what I found."

Fair enough. I did need to be something other than a total zombie the next day. I didn't want to risk being so exhausted I slept through the entire rising. I crawled into the bed and Ace threw himself down on one side of me while Griffin took the other. Tanner leaned over Ace to kiss me once, then twice. His lips were soft, and I smiled against him.

"I have the couch by the window. Caesar is patrolling the house once more, and then he'll take the place by the door. Rowan is in the corner over there. Being you, you can probably rise mid-day, so I wanted you to know how we're set up in case you wake up confused or not sure where you are."

That was sweet. "I'm going to try to make it to rising."

"Great." He nodded at me. "I know you like all the information you can get. You might sleep better knowing."

He squeezed my foot as he stepped away and Rowan entered the room. "I hate this place. It reminds me too much of my human childhood. He always hated home. Must be residual pain. Never mind. Griffin and Ace, you two were sneaky getting next to her tonight. I get it tomorrow, sending me off on that errand to check the locks. I was halfway there before I realized it."

Rowan didn't sound actually annoyed. If I wasn't mistaken, I could hear amusement in his voice as he threw himself down on the couch. It was a cute idea to feed me to sleep for a change, but I wasn't the one who usually had trouble knocking out. Caesar entered and, with unsteady movements, took his place on the couch.

"Love you," he called out before he squirmed around.

They were all in pain. Well, maybe not Ace, but the others. I patted Ace on the knee. "Tell you what? Let me feed all of them and then you feed me. That'll be a change but I want to try it. Or we feed each other, how about that?"

"Probably a good idea."

Griffin groaned. "We'll all get there, Mr. Daywalker.

Don't act all high and mighty because you're so used to it now."

I laughed. "It wasn't so long ago that this caused him pain, too. Actually, no, it was quite a bit ago? That's a human memory, so I guess it's been...almost a year?"

Time got funny in my head when I really stopped to consider how long ago things happened. Before death and after were complicated ideas.

Ace leaned back against the headboard. "I haven't struggled with it since that night. It surged me forward in my abilities. I might be able to go days."

"Fuck. Shut up before I break your nose." Griffin was in no mood for the conversation, and I tried not to find it amusing. Grumpy Griffin was really amusing to me.

I stared toward Caesar. He was really hurting. I could feel it in my bones, a distant pulse of pain like it was my own ache echoing through me. Why did I have this gift? Would we ever know? I sat next to him and then leaned down so he could reach my neck. He didn't even grumble, opening his mouth to bite down on me.

I closed my eyes. "Thank you for being there today even when it was hard."

He sighed, his whole body relaxing on the couch. In seconds, he was out cold. I lifted my head. Blood still trickled down my neck. It would have bothered me as a human; I could remember that it made her feel a general sense of yuckiness. My biggest concern currently was the idea I might waste it. The guys could smell it, the awake ones all shifted to watch me, like they couldn't wait for their turn to lick at the red liquid I knew they all craved.

I walked over to Rowan. He didn't like sharing blood in front of others, although he'd made no such indication when I'd first come back to life. "Do you want to do this someplace else?"

He shook his head. "Normally, yes, but I want to wake up in this room. So, no, here will do. Thank you for thinking of it. Maybe I can afford to be picky when this whole scenario is done. It's very human of me, I think. Vampires don't care about such matters."

"There are a lot of things about me that are very human, too." I extended my neck.

"Yes," Griffin said from the bed. "I'm aware. It's part of what we're going to talk about tomorrow. Neither of you are insane. None of us are. Try not to worry about it for the moment."

Rowan bit my neck, and I closed my eyes. If I let myself, I could fall asleep right there on top of him then spend the whole night sprawled over him like a limp doll.

But I wasn't done, so I forced my lids open. There wouldn't be rest until I finished. This was a change in how I did things but this needed to work. We had to be reciprocal and I was glad to see it could work that way too. Also, I needed to stay up and so I was glad to see I could.

Ace leaned back on his elbows. "You okay?"

I was and Rowan was out. But maybe I wasn't as tough as I pretended to be? I couldn't go endlessly without a feeding or sleep, much as I might like to think I could.

I left Rowan and went to Tanner, who reached for me, drawing me down next to him on his couch. "Think I could keep you right here? I'd love to cuddle all night. I could feed off you and you could pass out right here. Just give in."

"Hey," Griffin threw a pillow at him. "She sleeps on the bed. You lost out on it, so don't cheat now."

Tanner smirked. "But I'm a vampire. We're monsters. We cheat by nature." His mouth came down onto my already open wound and he sucked, hard. I moaned, pleasure flooding me. There really was a difference in how they fed and the effect it had on me. Caesar and Rowan hadn't elicited the same reaction with the few sips they'd stolen. It was about intent. Tanner meant to do what he did.

But it didn't last long. He was as exhausted as the rest of us, and none of us could follow through on what he started. I lifted my head. When we had time, he would pay for that little episode. Maybe I'd make him wait for it after I got him going sexually? We'd see. I had a hard time saying no to any of them, even for pretend.

And I didn't like to wait.

I rose and walked over to the bed.

Griffin shook his head. "You don't think we were going to let him turn you on and then leave you like that, did you?"

I climbed between them. "Seems like you might be a little bit tired for what he started." I smiled at Griffin.

He grinned at me, a goofy one for him, and not his usual smile. "Ace isn't stronger than me, despite what he might think. I'm the only one who really understands us now. I'm just about as tired as you are, my love." He kissed my chin. "Which means I have plenty of energy to give you what you need."

I shook my head. "How do you know how tired I am, Griffin?"

"I can feel it like you can feel it in me. We can all tell how you are most of the time. It would be annoying, if I didn't love you so much."

That word again. "You guys love slinging that about. She's not here to hear it. I love you guys too, but no matter how many times you say it, you can't make the human you didn't say it to hear what you should've said."

Griffin shook his head before he flipped me beneath

him. Ace rolled to his side, scooting close from the other side.

He winked at me as he spoke to Griffin. "I don't think she appreciates our dedication to making her come yet."

Ace bit me as Griffin pulled down my pants, giving him access to my underwear. I caught my breath, surprised. With a smooth move, Griff pushed my panties away and slipped his finger inside of me.

"Maci," his voice was in my ear, "I don't need you to feed me to sleep. I can go down any time I want to today. Feeding from you is not what I want right now. But I think—and Ace thinks—that we need to remind you that things can feel fantastic just because they can." He kissed my cheek, ever so gently. "Not to mention, as vampires, we can feel things more acutely than humans. So, this? It must just be rushing through your body."

He stroked my clit, and I drove myself against his hand. If they wanted to do this then I was game. As he fed from me from behind, Ace was hard.

"You don't pay attention to Ace feeding. He's just doing that, just feeding a little bit, because it enhances things for you. Sex and blood. Sometimes I want to separate the two, but that's really foolish because it either comes down to sex, blood or power with vampires. You hold all the power. So we can give you sex and we can play with blood, just like you can."

I always loved to hear Griffin speak. In every lifetime, I'd loved it. This wasn't different.

He pressed a second finger inside of me. I moaned. Yes, it was just what I needed. He was right. I craved the interaction, his touch. There was so much fucking pain all the time. There had to be pleasure.

"As for whether or not I can tell that girl I love her

despite the fact she's gone—you're still her, Maci, deep inside. You know it, and I know it, too."

Griffin bit down on me then. He wasn't gentle, not with his teeth or his fingers, which drove me wild. Every stroke brought me closer but not quite where I needed to be. *Fuck.* If they were going to drain me dry, so that I passed out, I wanted to come first. I knew they wanted my orgasm, too. Ace lifted his head, licking my wound closed.

"She's fighting it. Why would you do that, baby, when we know how badly you need to come? That's what we want to give to you. Come on his fingers, come screaming for us. You're so pretty when you give in."

His softly growled words were so fucking hot, but I didn't know what to do, because I did want to come. Badly. Right then. A surge of pleasure hit me, and I exploded around Griff's fingers, pressing against Ace as I did. Colors crossed over my vision, and I cried out, a hoarse sound I'd never heard myself make before. My body shook and Ace wrapped his arms around me, holding me tight. Griffin licked his bite mark closed.

"Good girl," Griff said as he peppered kisses over my cheeks. "Rest now, Maci. You need it more than anyone I know." He licked his lips. "Ace is going to give you just what you need and everything will get settled in the morning."

I could barely form words, but I managed, "You guys both need release."

Griff flipped me over so I faced Ace. "We're both fine. It feels good to be hard like this, pressed up against you. It makes me feel wanting, and I like it."

Ace extended his neck. "Feed, Maci. You haven't taken one break, not one, since you rose the first time. We thought we'd still be locked in the basement feeding you. We should have been, but we're out here and you're leading a war.

You're so hungry, you don't even know it anymore and now —whatever is happening—we can feed it. So take what you need, because it's ours to give you."

It was hard to argue with him when he made sense. I bit down on his neck, and I drank him in. They were right. I needed this, and them. Body and soul.

THE SUN SET and with it came the tug pulling at me to wake. I was pretty out of it, still happily unaware of my surroundings when the sounds of my guys talking finally made me lift my lids.

"She's pretty out of it." Rowan said as he ran his hands through my hair. "She needed to sleep. I'm glad you did whatever it was that the two of you did."

Ace sat down on the bed, despite the fact I'd never felt him leave it. "I'll always take care of Maci."

"Same for me." Griffin was across the room. "She's ours. We all managed to stay up yesterday, so that'll get easier and easier. Hopefully, there will come a day in the not too distant future when we can sleep at sunrise and rise at sun down without worrying about getting our asses kicked. In the meantime, I'm glad we have some protection. I think she's awake."

I raised my head. "Hard to sleep in with you guys talking over my bed."

"We missed you." Caesar walked over and kissed my cheek. "I wish we could leave you alone to rest, but I think you know we're very much at risk today. Soon, you'll get to lounge around if you want."

I didn't think that was exactly my nature, but I liked the thought just the same.

15

Griffin waited for me in one of the father s' offices. I didn't know which one; I just knew it wasn't Frederick's. Crossing the room and circling around the desk, I placed myself comfortably in his lap. "Okay. Tell me about your book."

He kissed my neck, his lips lingering. For a second, I thought he was going to bite down on me. Maybe he considered it, because his breath continued to stir the hairs at my nape for long after he placed the kiss, but at last he lifted his head.

"I love how you smell," he said, his warm eyes full of soft feelings for me.

I tugged his arms further around me, snuggling into his embrace. "I love how you smell, too, but if you want me to look at your prophecy book, it might be better if you didn't distract me."

"Right. Of course, you're the one who sat on my lap, which essentially means you're the one being the distraction, and you knew it."

He had always been the one to say things just as they

were, even when we'd both been humans. I blinked. He'd challenged me. And he played sports. I turned to look at him. "Sorry, strange memory to have. What did you ask me?"

"Was it something about you being human or humanity or something?"

He hit that one correctly on the first guess. "How did you know?"

Griffin held up and wiggled the book. "See? It's going to turn out my skill set does not make me completely useless to you."

I leaned back against him. "Were you under the impression that I thought you were useless? You're not. You're my Griffin. You're essential to me, and probably the smartest person I know."

"Thank you." He kissed my neck again. "This book is about vampire women. There aren't that many around, just you, Ace's mom. Your mom. Some others, but really not a lot. And I get the feeling the other women, maybe because they lived so long on the run, terrified, I feel like they haven't come into their own in the way that you are."

Was I? "Is that a compliment or do you really think that?"

"I really think it. I'm a vampire. We don't do compliments, just truth."

I shook my head. "You and I both know that's not true."

"I do, actually." He held up the book. "Because I read this. As I was saying, this book is about female vampires and the things you're able to do. It's fascinating. The thing you can do where you can see back into those other people's pasts? That is your vampire gift. We all have them. I can see far..."

I interrupted him. "Right. Caesar can smell ovulation."

"That's weird, right? Yes. He can do that." He laughed. "Anyway, yours is that you can see people's pasts. It's not some weird thing that happened because we're reincarnated or whatever. That's just bullshit. It read as bullshit to me when they told us about it, but then we all could see that past life?"

I nodded. "It doesn't make sense if it's just my gift. You saw the burning. You saw the whole thing, too." In fact, he'd been the first one to see it.

Griffin held up the book. "It's because we're your soul mates. There's more. Do you remember that your human-self used to have those dreams? The ones where you would sleepwalk?"

"Yes, but that was my dad feeding me. I didn't understand or remember then, but I do now."

He shook his head. "I don't mean that."

Griffin was so excited he pushed me off his lap, and I got up. He needed to pace. It was adorable, but he wouldn't like to hear that right that second.

"Yes, your dad did that, but you used to dream. We pulled you out of the woods once. Sorry, the humans did." He patted his head. "That slip will make sense in a second. The humans we were pulled you out of the woods."

I blinked. Yes, I had that memory. "Okay?"

"You can't tell me that was some kind of memory of that woman who died. It wasn't. It was someone else. You were moon seeking. It was sort of beautiful. The one who died in a fire? I've seen her whole life with the one whose memory I saw. She didn't do that."

My stomach clenched. "Who is it then and why do I have their memory?"

"It doesn't matter, sweetheart. The point is that you can encounter memories and we're so connected to you we can see them with you, sometimes. It's your vampire gift." He held up the book. "Very rare among females but lots of reference to them. Powerful vampires. I don't think Frederick or the fathers know anything about this. Yours doesn't. They all think it's about those people you saw. People we saw. And I think we only saw them because they told us we would. Because we read about them and told your human-self about them." Griffin sat back down and patted his knee. Did he want me to get back on his lap?

I walked back over and sat down on him. "Okay. So I could...what? Channel all the dead vampires?"

"Maybe if you tried hard enough."

I was absolutely not doing that. "Griffin, I don't want to carry around the memories of..."

"I don't think you need to worry about that. It seems that people with your gifts, they are also able to better access their past human lives. Again, through our connection to you, we can do that too, more than we should be able to."

Now it was my turn to get up. "Am I making us weaker? The humanity I can access? Is it hurting us?"

"No. I don't think so. I wouldn't want anything else. The way that I love you? The way that I know that they do? Maybe it's enhanced by the fact that our human selves did too. I can feel my love for you—intense, soul mate—and also gentle and easy. That was my human side. I get all of it."

I sat on the corner of the bed where I could regard him properly. "This is wonderfully interesting and I love it—in both the human and vampire way—but can it help us with this or is it just sort of good to know?"

"Oh, it'll help." He took my hand in his and kissed it. "He's never going to see you coming."

❧

Rowan leaned against the wall in the hallway when we came out. "You guys okay?"

"Yes. I think we may have just worked out a plan." I kissed his cheek. "Do you think we could round up some humans who want to be vampires and maybe get the process started?"

He blinked. "I don't know that we have the time to wait for an army to rise from the ground."

"No, we don't. What about just giving some of my blood?" I chewed on my bottom lip. "The humans will die, but we'll make them vampires. They want that. Can we do that?"

He nodded and then looked at Griffin. "Someone want to let me in on this plan or am I just rounding up servants from wherever they've fled? Do I get to know what we're doing?"

"You get to know." Was he feeling threatened, since he was the plan maker? "Griffin can fill you guys all in, and I'll go find the servants. I was one of them once, so maybe seeing me as a vampire will inspire them." I held up my hand. "I'll tell Caesar when we go. He won't want to be separated from me."

"None of us much care for the feeling." Rowan grabbed me and pinned me to the wall. His vampire was close to the surface, and my monster rose to greet him. I was used to seeing Tanner this way, not Rowan.

I stroked my finger over his bottom lip. "So now that we've said hello this way, I'll ask if everything's okay?"

"I'm struggling with my beast today. Some days it's a battle. Just a vampire thing. Maybe you haven't faced it yet, but mine is riding me. I miss the woman I love. Maybe Caesar could stay here, and I could go along as your protection tonight?"

I nodded. "Okay. Let's do that. Griffin, tell the others. I'll tell Rowan about the plan. I have to go find some servants."

Griffin tugged me against him. "I don't struggle with my vampire. We understand each other perfectly."

I rolled my eyes. "Liar."

"See? Human thing."

I EXPLAINED my plan to Rowan as we drove to a local motel to search for the servants. Without much money, if they weren't staying there, they were probably on the streets. Rowan drummed his fingers on the steering wheel in the parking space where we paused for a second, considering his options.

"It's a good plan, but it doesn't let me kill enough people." He closed his eyes. "Bad rising, probably because I stayed up yesterday."

I stroked my hand through his hair. "Should we see if Griffin's right?"

"What do you mean?"

I closed my eyes and thought about Rowan as a human. It was always a little bit like pushing through fog but at least I could do it, unlike others, it would seem. He'd looked at my human-self like she spun the world, and he'd worried about her, and the others, all the way to the end of his life. I pictured him smiling.

Rowan audibly caught his breath. "I can feel my human-self like he's here with me. For just a second, like I was both of us." He leaned back in his seat and blinked rapidly. "I feel calmer."

That was what I hoped would happen. "Griffin thought I could do that. Bring our humans to the surface. And you would get that from me because of our connection. Our soul mate connection."

He stared at me a long moment. "Our soul mate connection, that we formed as humans. Because we just did. Because you were going to be a vampire too, and the vampire I was going to be recognized the vampire in you. Not because we're long dead people. But because we're these people."

I nodded. "It feels right to me. Doesn't it feel right to you?"

"It does." He kissed my lips, gently. "Thank you for reminding me of who he was. I lose him sometimes, and he was a nice kid."

"He was."

I felt them before I saw them. My other guys were all there. Caesar tapped on my window, and a second later, I rolled it down. "None of us want to wait at home. All of us are perfectly capable of defending you as easily as Rowan here is." He glared at Rowan. "Maybe some of us would be better at it."

He'd always find me, that was what Caesar promised, and he had proven that over and over.

Rowan shook his head. He was calm but I was sure he could be angry again in a hot second. If that happened, I'd leave them to it. I had many problems in life but solving their macho shit was not one of them.

"If you need a reminder of my power, Caesar, I'd be happy to demonstrate it."

I got out of the car. They could sort it out. They'd been pretty much brothers since birth. I walked toward the motel. "Which one of you can cause trances and mind erasure the best?"

It wasn't something we'd done since I rose. Maybe I was

the best, but I'd never done it and it was not the time I felt like practicing. Tanner was quickly on my left, Ace on my right.

Tanner grinned at me. "They don't really think they're stronger than me, right?"

"You're all dwarfed by me." Ace shrugged. "But I don't feel like showing it off all the time."

Griffin laughed, catching up. "Okay. I'd never suggest that I could beat any of you in a physical fight, but I'm smarter than the rest of you. This is my plan we're enacting. Go ahead and beat each other. I win in the end."

"Did I miss the part where you all woke up this ridiculous today? I'm stronger than the rest of you." I might not be, but I'd lead with that.

Tanner through his arm around me. "You absolutely are. My vampire thinks your vampire could kick our collective asses. He's been waiting for you since the change. The second we met you as humans we were connected. I think it was that vampire blood speaking to each other."

I cupped his cheek. "Then I guess it's a good thing our fathers believed in prophecies."

Right then, I believed we could pull off Griffin's plan, but it was going to take finding some women who wanted to be vampires. In the end, I would make them vamps, if that was what they still wanted.

"Hi," said a voice I hadn't expected to hear. I recognized it, though, instantly from a different world. "I see you have finally found us."

Wanda. She saved me because Ace's father asked her to do it. I knew why he asked her, but I wasn't sure why she'd done it on her end. Once, Wanda had been a servant, but she was one of the few to get out. She owned a bar they all hung out in, near where my human-self grew up. She kept the human alive when she almost died, even giving her a place to live for a time.

I hadn't seen her since, but now she was there.

"Wanda," I walked toward her, hands outstretched. "I didn't expect you to be here."

She waved her hand. "I'm thinking about leaving, but I hoped to see you again. I don't know how they think they're going to beat you, with you being fated or whatever."

I didn't know if I should correct her assumption or not. I wasn't fated, I was talented, but maybe we'd leave them with some misinformation. I didn't want to have the whole argument about whether or not I was fated, so it might be better if she thought I was.

"I'm glad to see that you're fine. I should thank you for the kindness you showed the human I used to be." Even if I didn't know why she offered it, which was going to bother me until I got answers. "Was it because you knew I was fated?"

She nodded. "I was close with Ace's mother. Have they met yet?"

"Badly." I shrugged, then I touched Ace's arm. "And not something we're going to discuss. Ever." I nodded to her. "Did you want to be a vampire?"

She took a step toward the door of her hotel room. "When I was young and beautiful, maybe. When I could have spent eternity looking like all of you, I likely would have said yes. Who would want to be eternally like this?"

I thought Wanda was beautiful. Actually, I'd never given it any thought since my rebirth, and it wasn't something I'd have dwelled on presently, either. What did I care about physical looks? There was blood, sex, and power. The rest of it was nothing, at least for the moment.

But my human-self thought she was beautiful. She lived

a long, hard life, and the map of that time was written on her face. When I looked at Wanda, I could see all the things that happened in my human life. Wanda lived and she would die—in her human cycle, if we didn't interfere with it.

"We don't actually care about such things. There are other factors that make us attractive as vampires, like power." I stepped back. "But you've certainly earned the right to change your mind, if that is what you want. Thank you, again. I don't know what would have happened to me, if you hadn't intervened."

Griffin stared at me, adding logic. "You'd have died and risen. Your father had been feeding you for some time."

"Well, then, we wouldn't have had the time we had together, not with me as a human basically being your paramour and you guys as vampires not at all sure what to do with that little human. Is there anything we can do for you, Wanda?"

She sighed. "Don't die. I like hanging out with the vampire crowds the way that I do. I'm sick in the head. And I hate Frederick. I'd rather things go forward with you all in charge."

I didn't want to be in charge. When we were done, we intended to go back to how it had been in the past. Vampires would make families and not be dictated to by insane leaders who had no business leading anything at all.

"If it were me, Wanda, I'd get away from the vampires. Far, far away." That was the absolute truth. "If you need anything from me, ever, I'm here for you. Anything at all you need."

She stared at me, and I hugged her. It wasn't natural for me, but I did it anyway. "I mean it. Anything."

"Wanda," Caesar said from behind me. I guessed he and Rowan either sorted out their shit or paused it. "You kept her alive until I could find her. Thank you. If she had been reborn before then, I'm not sure we would be where we are now. Rowan sent her away with no help."

I knew the roaring response was going to come before it ever did. "Because I was not informed about her situation. If I had known human-Maci needed help, she would have gotten help. Or she would have stayed with us. I'm not a monster." He lowered his voice. "None of us are, despite what they told us."

So much pain resonated in his voice, I had to pause. The servants could wait a second. I turned toward him. "She wasn't upset with you when she died. Not even a little bit."

They didn't get closure with that Maci. She'd been basically out of it when she died, and when I showed up, I hadn't wanted or needed what she had emotionally from them. I loved them, they loved me—that part was easy, and there was no doubt of it, but they still lived with the pain of what hadn't been done for that version of me.

I thought about how much she loved each of them. Not just as humans, but she'd loved them as vampires, too. The way it had felt when Caesar showed up—she'd equally hated and loved him until quickly that hate vanished. He was like a gift presented to her from the universe. The way he had cared about her, it changed his whole life for her. She hadn't experienced anything else like it in her whole life or any of her other remembered lives.

And then Griffin had come. *Brilliant, smart and confusing.* He'd hurt her, but then he fixed it. Griffin never let her down. He stayed with her, talked to her, made such an effort that she felt the way he loved her even when he never said it. He mended her heart.

Tanner sought her out when he couldn't even speak. He treasured her immediately, as though no time passed between them. Instantly, they'd been back in love. She wanted to wrap herself up in him and never let go. What was more, he might have let her if she tried it.

Ace had been so wounded and frightened, but he'd switched immediately to protection. He'd amazed her, enthralled her, and made her believe there might be a future for them despite the odds. He battled for her every step of the way until she died. She felt his devotion in her cells, in her heart, in her soul.

Rowan returned to her last, but it had been no less intense of a reunion. He'd challenged her, and they clawed at each other like animals, angry and desperate for each other. But he was willing to destroy everything for her, and she knew that he loved her. He was desperate for her love and attention, and she wanted to give him the world of love, if he would accept it.

I sent the thoughts to the surface of my brain, hoping my men would feel it. One of them made a sound like a gasp and then silence. They all felt it; she loved them with everything inside of her. They needed to know, so they could experience that love the way she would have wished it.

No more questions. No more doubts.

I stepped back. "Okay?"

"Maci." It was Caesar who finally spoke, his voice rough. "You just had to know."

I turned my back on them. If they needed time to digest what I showed them, that was fine, I'd understand. But I would finish what I needed to while I still could. They didn't leave me to do it alone. Instead, I was instantly surrounded. I planned on bothering the front desk clerk, but instead I turned to Wanda, who stared at us with confusion evident on her features. Yes, she would have no idea what just transpired.

And I preferred it that way.

"Where are the servants?"

She pointed behind her. "Three rooms, fifty-two, fifty-three, and fifty-four."

They had to all be sharing, but it still meant a lot of them to be sharing just three rooms.

I knocked on fifty-two. After a moment, the door swung open. Five women stared wide-eyed at me. I probably looked pretty scary to them, not only as a vampire, but who knew what Frederick told them about me.

Or maybe they'd known me as a servant, and who knew what they'd think about me then.

I didn't specifically recognize any of the servants, but that was fine. "Hello, I'm Maci. I want to talk to you guys about moving forward with some things."

It was stupid of me not to realize they might want to kill me. Frederick did, and they were loyal to him—stupidly so, but loyal just the same.

The woman at the front of the crowd firmed up her lips then launched herself at me like she could take off my head. She'd never be able to hurt me, but it didn't matter. I wasn't prepared for her, and she would have at least knocked me over, and who knew what she would attempt next?

But she never got the chance. Instead, she landed with a crash against the wall, pinned to it on the other side of the room. She screamed out in pain, and I whirled around to see Rowan standing with his arms crossed over his chest.

"No one is going to fuck with Maci. I don't know what you've been told or what you believe, and I don't even particularly care. You're going to listen to Maci. If you don't want to do what she says, fine, you don't have to, but you'll make no moves to hurt her. Never again. Do I make myself clear?"

The others nodded their heads fast, and one of them

spoke, "I don't know why Kristen did that. The rest of us would never hurt Maci. You're all vampires. You're gods." She seemed to regard me for a second. "And goddesses."

I got to my feet and stared where Kristen flailed against the wall, an angry moth with claws. *Well, that isn't going to be helpful.*

"Rowan?"

He shook his head. "She's going to stay there for a long while. I'm deciding whether or not I'll kill her. Don't give her any more attention in the meantime, Maci. She's handled."

Okay. I would leave that alone for the moment. I didn't know Kristen, and I didn't appreciate being attacked. Maybe spending time against the wall would be good for her.

"Let's start again. I'm Maci , and I know some of you want to be vampires. All of you probably. Why else would you be doing what you're doing?" I smiled. "Maybe I can make you one."

16

Tanner turned out to be the best at putting humans in a trance. Hilarious, considering he couldn't talk without me, but he was so good at it, he could actually make them go blurry without words.

"Okay, little human," Tanner said to one girl, sounding amused. "You aren't going to remember any of this, but when I say go, you are going to drink Maci's blood. It won't taste good to you at first, but trust me, it's delicious. An acquired taste. When I say stop, you'll stop and go straight back to your hotel room. Tomorrow, you will find Frederick and those vampires. They will feed on you, but you won't remember *any* of this."

They might kill her, but lucky for her, she would get what she thought she wanted. For that reason, my guilt for her and the others could be minimized. Besides, if the guilt really started to bother me, I could just let my monster take control and I could feel nothing about it at all.

So interesting to be a vampire who could control that. And my past human-self.

All of it was very loud in my head all the time.

"Yes," she said and nodded.

I elbowed Tanner. "*Little human*?"

"I don't remember her name," he explained with a shrug. Neither did I. Maybe my monster was already nice and close after all.

"Would you?" I lifted my wrist toward him and his eyes flared red. Without answering aloud, he took a long, hard bite. When he lifted his head, my blood dripped down his mouth. I grinned at him. He was ridiculously cute.

Instead of focusing on my men, I dug into the task at hand. I let that nameless human and so many other of her friends feed from me. The night spun on, feeling endless to me.

By the time the last one finished, I was past ready to be done. Although I gained no pleasure in them feeding from me, my guys seemed to have a vastly different experience. Perhaps because all of the servants had been women, and they watched me embrace each one? Whatever the reason, their reaction seemed akin to them watching porn.

Caesar held me from behind, his cock pressed against my ass firmly. His boldness and his breath near my ear said that if I just gave him permission, he'd fuck me from behind right then and there.

It wasn't happening. Rowan's phone dinged and he nodded, trying to focus past his reaction. "Your dad says everything is good back at their location. His spies say Frederick's people are in chaos right now. They had a terrible rising and are still trying to get things fixed before the sun comes up again. You scared him with the flames. He knows you remembered."

I closed my eyes, not wanting to think of my death in flames again. Of course, him admitting that meant he thought I was some sort of chosen one. Which I wasn't, but we could play on his fears when I brought them to their knees at the next rising. I'd be there, and they wouldn't even know it. From that moment onward, I'd be inside of all of them just waiting for the right moment to show them what I could do.

We got back in the car and made our way home, leaving the servants to sleep. Likely, they'd be feeling pretty confused the next day. Wanda wouldn't say anything, I knew. She was trustworthy, but I was pretty sure Caesar gave her a little vampire suggestion just to be sure she kept quiet while we'd been busy.

It was quiet in the car, but the overall mood remained light. We might not have won yet, but we found hope.

"Maci!" a woman greeted me as I got out of the car. It took me a second to realize it was my mother. *Well, I made Ace deal with his. My turn.*

Ace reached for me then cupped my cheek. His meaning was clear: *You aren't alone.* I stared at my mother with his warmth surrounding me like a cape for a second then stepped out of his embrace.

"Want to take a walk?" I asked her.

She nodded. "Very much."

"Good. Come." I left my guys behind. The sun would be out soon and there was no way they would let me get far away, but maybe they'd give me some privacy for this partic-ular conversation. She wasn't likely to hurt me.

We walked for a few minutes, the breeze cool against my face, before I asked, "How close to rising can you stay up?"

Her smile was fast. "I can stay up for days. Where do you think you get it from? Your father took years to get where I was in months. You're even faster, from what I understand."

Well, that was interesting. I hadn't considered vampire

genetics, and I didn't have the time to deal with them in the moment.

My voice broke a little, but I got out the words. "You left me with a drug addict. Well, you left *her*. The previous me." I might as well get the truth out there fast, while I had the chance to say the words I held like wounds in my chest from her life. "And she wasn't kind. She would leave Maci, and sometimes she even tried to force men on her."

We were already pretty pale as vampires, but her face went chalky. "I didn't know. Your father...he never told me. I asked about her regularly, and he always said she was okay. I would have come. I always wanted to come, to check on her for myself, but he told me not to ever go near you." Tears leaked from her eyes. "He said we had to stay away for your own good. You're the one who was prophesied."

I almost dropped the bad news. *No prophecy mattered more than your own kid.* But she looked at me with such disastrous pain in her eyes, I couldn't say it. Maybe we'd both been the victims of things beyond our control. The politics of vampires just fucked with us all.

"Look..." I realized I didn't need to keep poking at her. If she hadn't known, she did now. There would be problems with my father because he lied to her, and maybe that was between them. The human I was had died. I could feel that version of Maci, but no amount of yelling at my mother would bring her back. "I'm okay. Obviously, I'm a vampire now. Whatever happened when I was a human, I can't change it. When this is over, let's see if we can get to know each other. Maybe we can be friends."

She wiped at her eyes, her lip trembling. "He always said I could have my daughter back when she was reborn. I should have known it would never be that simple. I just wanted it to be because it was so hard to give over the baby.

To hand her over like she was a tool and not just a beautiful human baby that I'd birthed. They killed me the day that you were born. When I woke up, you were all I could think about. No one would even tell me where they took you for almost a year. I didn't even know where they'd sent you." She took my hand in hers. "I'm sorry. If friends is what I can have, then I'll look forward to that. Maybe I could even meet the guys who are following us around like I might try to stake you."

"I'm very lucky in my soul mates." I touched her arms, staring into eyes like my own, but nothing like my own at the same time. "There's a fight coming. I don't know if it'll be big or small, but it will be tomorrow."

Her eyes flared red, the warrior in her grin familiar. "I wouldn't miss it."

I ROSE the next day knowing our wait was over. Around me, the guys all still slept, their even breathing sounding like home. I could hardly remember our going to bed. The joyful sexiness of the night before hadn't happened, as I'd been lost in my thoughts. *Humans and vampires. Babies and decisions. Soul mates and prophecies.*

My men seemed equally lost in ruminations. We were soul mates but also individuals, and none of us really had time to process any of it as it happened. I could bring on their humans, I could influence their powers, but I couldn't be in their heads all the time. That was probably a good thing, as it wouldn't be fair to never give them time to be alone.

Why was I up before sunrise, then? I didn't know. The feeling I got before a battle wasn't there, no buzzing in my brain. We weren't about to be under attack. I slept between Tanner and Caesar last night, and their warmth cocooned me still. Neither had roused. I got out of bed, carefully rolling free of their limbs, then walked to the other side of the house to look out the window.

It was the middle of the day.

I knew what I had to do. The certainty of it filled me with motivation. I couldn't stand still a moment longer. I got dressed quickly then took a brief second to pause. It was time to play my role, but I didn't know if I had to wake the guys. They'd find me when they roused. They always would, and it might be cruel not to wake them. I shook my head. Why was I worrying about it? I knew what to do. The guys would want to be awake. End of story.

I crawled back onto the bed. "Caesar," I whispered, but he didn't wake. I had to try, so I turned toward Tanner and tugged his arm, calling his name.

I saved Ace for last. He was the best with the daytime waking, yet even he didn't stir right away. Finally, his eyes opened. He blinked at me, his monster right on the surface of his gaze. I smiled at him. "Awake?"

He blinked. "Sure. What's wrong?"

"We have to go there now. I can't explain it, but I have to be there now. I can't wake the others, although I tried. I thought about just leaving, but I worried you guys would never forgive me." My voice shook. "I need you to come, Ace. Please. I have to go now."

He took my cheeks in his hands, comfort in his touch. "You didn't feed before you went to bed, Maci. I'll tell you what? I want you to feed right now. If you still want to go after you feed, we'll go. I'll figure out how to wake the others then we'll go. Okay?"

His words sounded reasonable. *Yes, I'll be calmer after I*

feed. He extended his neck and I bit down on him, his familiar flavor rushing over my tongue, tasting like mine. Warm and solid. His power rushed through me. I closed my eyes.

~

A HAND STROKED MY HAIR. "She was hysterical, didn't seem like herself. I think her anxiety was through the roof, very nearly to the point of being frantic," Ace whispered. "I'm not waking her a second before she rouses on her own."

Caesar kissed my cheek. "She's up. Slowly, baby. You did the right thing. No way did anything have to happen at noon, but what the fuck is the matter with me that I didn't wake up? I can't have my girl needing me and not even budge."

"We're baby vampires," Griffin said, looking disgusted with himself as he sighed. "Whatever we're pretending, we're still young. After today, maybe we can rest on a more regular schedule."

I lifted my head. "Thank you, Ace. I was obviously...off."

"It's always going to be my pleasure to take care of you."

I kissed his chin before I moved over to feed Tanner. When I would have given him my neck, he offered his instead. *Really?* I bit down and drank from him without thinking about it too much. I didn't want to drain him, just to give him his voice back. Still, I took a longer minute than I usually would.

When I pulled back and closed the wound, he kissed me on my chin, and then trailed the kiss up to my lips when they were free. "I'm sorry I didn't wake. Next time, just feed from me while I'm asleep. I give you permission, eternal consent."

"I didn't know I needed to feed until Ace told me to do it. Then I suddenly knew, but I still didn't realize how out of it I was."

Tanner smiled at me. "You had to have been starving. We need to know that you have to feed even if you think you don't before bed. Every night. You *have* to feed."

"I think you're right, but for now, I need to go kill the psychos holding up our life. And I feel smart and ready to do it."

"Good." He kissed the end of my nose. "Thank you, Ace," he prompted.

"Yes, thank you, Ace." Rowan hugged him. "My weakness continues to plague me. Daytime is such a problem."

I shook my head. "It turned out I was the one who was off. I don't even know at this point what woke me, but we need to see if our plan is working out. The servants should be heading over there shortly."

"Right." Griffin got off the bed where he had lounged, looking far too gorgeous. He threw me a playful wink. "The next time you wake up in a state, just feed off me. It's fine."

That was absolutely not going to happen. "That just doesn't feel consensual, even with prior permission."

I was pretty sure that if I ever woke up in that state again, I might obey his order anyway. If Ace couldn't help me or couldn't wake up...the whole situation seemed weird, and I didn't like not knowing why it happened.

The drive to check on whether our plan was working took very little time. My father, mother and Ace's father were already there, binoculars trained on the scene below. "Remind me why we sent them in there to let them feed on them again?" My father turned to me. "Oh, and if you intend to throw me under the bus with your mother, a warning in advance would be nice.

"Are we setting up a parental relationship I'm unaware of?" I shrugged, giving him an eye roll. "You dug that hole. Vampires don't lie, but you did for *years*. At least I know where I got that little ability from, too."

Ace's dad laughed. "You realize she's exactly like you."

"I'm starting to," my father answered, his expression torn between amusement and annoyance.

Caesar slid close, his arms wrapping around me from behind as he addressed my father. "Don't ever criticize anything she does. I mean, *ever*. If you do, we're going to have a problem."

I had to bite my lip to resist laughing. His threat was, of course, ridiculous but I loved that he felt that way. Everyone should have someone who thought they were basically perfect in their life to love them. I snuggled further into his embrace. *If only we could just stay like this for a while.*

But there were the servants, and my entire plan, left to consider. "I'm not going to explain any details until things are done. Then I'll fill you in, I promise." I finally answered my father's question. "If you don't like my plan, you're welcome to use your own."

Griff stroked a finger down my cheek. "Ready for what's next?"

I guessed we would see. I had no idea if I was ready, since I'd either be able to do what Griffin told me I could or I wouldn't. In either case, I really preferred our plan over one where I was a prophesied super vampire who came to save them all. I wasn't the scarred-forehead wizard of vampires. Abruptly, I remembered those books, surprised to find a human memory that didn't make me feel horrified for the Maci before. *She really liked to read.*

"Maybe I am ready for what's next." I kept my gaze on the servants. Sure enough, the vampires were feeding. They looked hungry. They'd been kept nice and cushy by Frederick, so it had been a long time since their food didn't just appear in front of them. They had to be so relieved to see their servants arrive.

"About what percentage of them have fed?" I asked, shooting a look at my father. "Hazard a guess."

"Eighty to ninety percent."

That was better than I thought we'd get. The servants should be passing out from blood loss. If I hadn't fed them, they would be. It was a good thing that my father had done that for me for years or I wouldn't have made it through my human years with the feeding I did.

"Okay. I'm going down." An alarm jangled inside of me, telling me it was time. Time to end Frederick and his top followers, then we'd see if there was anything left to save in the others. They'd all been deceived for a long time. If they could get with the new program, they didn't have to die. I wouldn't even be the one making the decision. I'd leave that to the Betrayer, who happened to be my father. He'd been fighting them—albeit for his own reasons—a lot longer than me, after all.

A hand grabbed my arm—my mother. "I told you I'd be here. Even if *someone* tried to fool me about the timing and I almost missed it." She shot my father a disgusted look, and he glared back at her. I could feel the tension of their ongoing fight, and knew it had to be about me and what he had and hadn't done for years. I figured they would work it out one day. It was a soul mate thing; we forgave each other. Even as a baby vampire, I knew that much.

"Thank you," I told my mother. "I'm glad to have you. More than glad. I...I appreciate that you got here despite obstacles as large as the ones my father must have thrown at you."

Her smile was a little wobbly, and I squeezed her finger-tips. We had a lot of work to do to mend our relationship, or maybe build one.

But I had things to say to my guys. Things that I should have said before we left the house. I turned away from her, surprised at the urgency when I didn't even realize I needed to talk to them until that moment.

"Guys, could we talk for a second, please? Follow me over here."

I think my distress must have been in my tone, because they all joined me. Still out of sight from our enemies, I ensured our privacy before I started to speak. "I don't know if this is going to work, and I don't know if they're going to kill me if it fails."

"They won't." Rowan's eyes flared red. "I won't allow it."

He still thought he held some control over the universe. I loved that about him, even if I couldn't believe in it myself. "Okay. Let's hope it doesn't come to that, but if it does, and there is some kind of reincarnation afterward, some sort of choice in all of this...I will always find you. Okay? I will always be yours. This was the best bit of luck in the universe that I found you, and I want to let you know I will always find you."

Ace shot Griffin a look but the other didn't respond. I didn't know what it meant, but I figured they could explain later.

"Don't worry about what you can't control in this," Tanner took my hand. "Just do what you can. We believe you can do this."

My love who could sometimes not find his voice's words still rang in my ears as I walked toward the group forming around Frederick. Vampires were supposed to be so fearless, but I didn't feel brave right then. Instead, I was a girl in way over my head trying to pull off a plan we just threw together. I tried living my life as a human, and they didn't let me. I wasn't asking permission this time. Now I just had to take control and get this man out of my way.

He pushed forward, fury in his eyes. "You."

Well...that was articulate. I could say something but that wasn't the point. It was better to show everyone what I knew they needed to see. It was hard to deny the evidence in front of their eyes. The vampires who couldn't change their minds about him were too far lost. We'd know soon.

My blood beat inside their veins, each and every one of them, even if they didn't know it yet. I'd given it to them. Those I shared my blood with could be manipulated to be affected by my power. I lifted my head to the sky, and I let them in. All of them. The presences I ignored, the ones that sometimes woke me from sleep, both as a human and now as a vampire. I hadn't even realized until that moment what the voices were.

But Griffin had known.

He'd always known.

We carried our ghosts around with us. All of us did. Maci the human lived with them constantly. Fear was her ghost. Loneliness. Uncertainty. As a vampire, I'd always have those, too. Maci the human was one of my ghosts. The memories of those who came before me would also always live in my mind. I could feel all of them. Frederick couldn't feel his, but I could.

I let them *all* in.

Rowan touched my back. It was the last thing I noted before I released them all, freeing them like butterflies hatched from the cocoon of my chest. The memories of all the people Frederick and betrayed and killed, one by one, they flew out of me. I started with the women—most of these men would forever live half-lives because they believed a man who cheerfully killed all the women who could have been their soul mates. He'd done that, and they'd let him. The women who had been killed for carrying girl babies, each life snuffing out and taking love and possibility with them. The women he'd killed because it was funny to him. The women who wanted to be vampires but never would because he'd lied to them.

It wasn't just the women because I also released the memories of the men. Of his followers, who he simply rid himself of because he could. The ones who dared to question him, the ones who got in his way—over and over, I let them see. They thought they were *safe* with him? How foolish! He might have hidden that side of himself, but he couldn't hide it anymore. As I showed the others, he could see himself, too. Every memory wanted to greet him, but they said hello to me instead. I let them have their say with everyone.

The last thing I shared was myself. I showed them my death, the meaningless death of a nothing human. One he tormented and beat until the life was pounded out of her. It wasn't how vampires used to live, nor how they had to live going forward. Those memories I'd been forced to endure came next. The ones of how it could be, when they lived a good life. Powerless in the end, but I wasn't. Didn't the vampires in our time want a chance at something like that? I let them see how Frederick wanted to rape her, how all of it happened because he had been denied by a woman who didn't want to have sex with him.

Finally, I let it go. I panted, sweat beading across my face and neck. I burned a lot of energy, and it wasn't something I ever tried to do before, especially not to that degree. Touches of it, while sharing memories with my guys over the last weeks. "As a human, I was asked to consider a scenario about depleting oxygen. About who deserved to live and who deserved to die. If anyone." That had been another time Griffin knew things. "I don't have room anymore for anyone who thinks this is okay. We're vampires. We love our monsters. We don't let them control the world." I looked at Tanner. He would understand the difference. "The strongest of us know to shut it down if it's too much. Maybe you forgot that, Frederick, but I didn't."

I didn't need matches to set him on fire. I had Rowan and Caesar. Frederick never even saw them coming. Ace lifted him in the air, and Rowan flung him backward. *Why bother with flames outside when I have it inside of me?* The power that I needed welled up.

"You burned her to death. I'll be kinder to you."

As he'd done with the vampire who wanted to kill me when I'd been a human, Griffin staked him. One second Frederick was there, and the next, he was gone.

I turned my head. "All of them."

Rowan grinned at me. "Like your boss?"

"Like my boss." Rowan showed he could do it to a human, so I had no doubt he could handle it with the vampires, too.

There they all were. All the fathers. The ones who tortured my men as children. I wasn't putting up with them anymore.

One by one, they went down. They didn't even try to resist. The memories I sent out changed them all. Struck them, but for some people, it was too late for redemption. It was time they all remembered their humans.

Another gift I can give them.

I closed my eyes. I'd probably be spent afterward, but it

would be worth it. *That's just fucking fine. If I fall, Caesar will catch me. He always does.*

"Maci..." Griffin called my name, and I lifted my eyelids.

"Did I faint?" We were in the back of the car, clearly heading away from the scene I'd just made.

He nodded. "More like collapsed, but it's fine. What you did was impressive as hell. More than I could've imagined, and I gotta confess something to you."

"*Now* he has to confess?" Tanner laughed. "What's the point now?"

"What's that?" I asked and sat up. All the guys were in the car with me.

Griffin admitted, "I lied."

He lied? "Well, we all do. It's okay. The whole *vampires don't lie* thing is nonsense."

"I mean, I lied when I said you weren't prophesized. Of course you were. I made up the rest. You didn't like being destined. The second I told you that you weren't, you did what you were destined to do."

I stared at him. "Griffin."

"I know."

I started to laugh. It was a beautiful night outside, the moon hanging large and orange in the sky. "Stop the car."

"Did you break her?" Caesar asked as we got out of the car, me still clutching my sides in humor. "I don't think she should be laughing about this."

Rowan and Ace were next to me, and Ace rubbed my back. It was the latter who spoke first. "What are we doing out here, Maci?"

A field in front of us swayed heavy with corn, so I walked toward it. "We're going to be vampires. We won't worry about prophecy right now. I'm hungry, so catch me and let me feed."

With that, I ran like my life depended on it, because it did. The rest of my life. It was Tanner who caught me in seconds, but he threw me to Rowan. Tanner wanted to be his monster for a while yet, which I understood. So did I. And, if Rowan's red glinting gaze was any indication, so did he. I'd deal with Griff's lies some other time. I wasn't a destiny.

I was a vampire named Maci, and I just won.

It was time for blood. *My trials are over.*

OTHER BOOKS BY REBECCA ROYCE...

Contemporary Romance

Redheads:

Redhead on the Run

Redheaded Redemption

Real Men Love Redheads (coming soon)

Reverse Harem Story (completed series)

Unconventional

Unexpected

Undeniable

Kiss Her Goodbye (completed series)

Hard Truths

Dark Truths

Deadly Truths

Stupid Boys (writing with C.R. Jane)

Stupid Boys

Dumb Girl

Crazy Love (coming soon)

Science Fiction Romance:

Wings of Artemis (completed series)

Kidnapped By Her Husbands

Deal Breaker

Throne Taker

Stranded Hearts (writing with Vivien Jackson)

The Girl Who Fell From The Sky

The Girl Who Crossed The Stars (coming soon)

Through the Gates (writing with Skye MacKinnon)

Purgatory City

Infernal Land (coming soon)

Paranormal Romance:

Trials of Blood

Servant

Paramour

Flame

Last Hope (completed series)

Tradition Be Damned

Past Be Damned

Destiny Be Damned

Compassion Be Damned

Future Be Damned

Dragon Wars (completed series)

Forever

Eternal

Always

Evermore

Endless

Wards and Wands (completed series)

Hexed and Vexed

Curse Reversed

Meow, Baby (novella, co-written with Ripley Proserpina)

Tragic Magic

Why Yes, There are Witches (novella)

Safe Haven

Everywhere and Nowhere

Dimension X (coming soon)

More coming soon....

Soul Bound

Prisoner of the Dragons

More coming soon....

Shadow Promised

Strange Days

Weird Nights

Bizarre Years

More coming soon...

The Westervelt Wolves (completed series)

Her Wolf

Summer's Wolf

Wolf Reborn

Wolf's Valentine

Wolf's Magic

Alpha Wolf

Angel's Wolf

Darkest Wolf

Lone Wolf

Fallen Alpha

Alpha Rising

Alpha's Strength

Alpha's Sacrifice

Alpha's Truth

Alpha Enticing

Hidden Alpha (coming soon)

Cascade (completed series)

Haunted Redemption

Phoenix Everlasting

Fragility Unearthed

Persuasion Enraptured

The Swamp Princess (completed series)

Hidden

Pursued

Caught

The Coveted (writing with Ripley Proserpina)

Eyes in the Darkness

Voices in the Darkness

Return to the Darkness

Prison Princess (part of the Prison Princess world, writing with CoraLee June)

Young Adult/New Adult Urban Fantasy/Post-Apocalyptic:

The Warrior (completed series)

Initiation

Driven

Subversive

Redemption

Justice

Warrior World (spin off of The Warrior, completed series)

Deacon

Micah

Jason

Fantasy Romance:

Life of the Chosen

The Ritual (coming soon)

The Storm (writing with Ripley Proserpina) **completed series.**

Lightning Strikes

Thunder Rolling

The Deluge

Addalee Ackers

The Hunted (coming soon)

Stand Alone Titles